F. Ritchie

Easy Greek Grammar Papers

F. Ritchie

Easy Greek Grammar Papers

ISBN/EAN: 9783337387471

Printed in Europe, USA, Canada, Australia, Japan

Cover: Foto ©Andreas Hilbeck / pixelio.de

More available books at **www.hansebooks.com**

EASY

GREEK GRAMMAR PAPERS

BY

F. RITCHIE, M.A.

The Beacon, Sevenoaks

LONGMANS, GREEN, AND CO.

LONDON, NEW YORK, AND BOMBAY

1896

ABERDEEN UNIVERSITY PRESS.

PREFACE.

THESE Papers, which are progressive in difficulty, have been systematically compiled in such a way as to include most of the Accidence and Syntax of which a knowledge is likely to be required by the Lower and Middle Forms.

It is suggested that the Papers may with advantage be used for *vivâ-voce* practice in Grammar, as well as in the ordinary way.

EXPLANATORY.

1. Weak Aorist = 1st Aorist;

   Strong Aorist = 2nd Aorist;

   and so with Perfects Act. and Future Passive.

2. Principal Tenses =

   Pres., Future, Aorist and Perf. Active,

   Perf. and Aorist Passive; so,

   λύω, λύσω, ἔλυσα, λέλυκα, λέλυμαι, ἐλύθην.

3. ττ = σσ; so, τάττω = τάσσω.

1. Write out Imperf. Indic. Act. of βάλλω.

2. 1st Sing. Fut. Indic. Act. of βοηθέω, ὀρθόω, θύω, ἀπατάω.

3. Decline in Singular ὥρα, λύπη, γλῶττα (see Explan. 3).

4. Acc. and Gen. Sing. of δῆλος and ἐλεύθερος.

5. Write in Capitals γ, δ, η, λ, ρ, ξ, θ.

6. Parse ποιήσειν, ἔφευγες, ἐπείθου, λύοντι.

7. Translate—ἡ καλὴ γυνή. καλή ἡ γυνή. ἡ γυνὴ καλή.

8. Translate—Out of the house ; into the land ; in the village ; the gates of the city.

2.

1. Write out Imperf. Indic. Middle of πείθω.

2. 1st Sing. Aorist Indic. Act. of σιωπάω, πληρόω, φιλέω.

3. Parse πεμπέτε, ἐλείπεσθε, κωλύοντος.

4. Nom. and Gen. Sing. of δόξῃ, υἱ▮ν, σοφίαν, τοξότας.

A

5. Name the Hard and the Soft Vowels.

6. Greek for—7, 11, 20, 4th, 6th.

7. Translate—οἱ ἐν τῇ ἀγορᾷ πολῖται. ἐπί-
στενον αὐτῷ. ἐπίστευσαν αὐτοῖς. μετὰ τὴν μάχην.

8. Translate—The arms are in the city; the
road from the village; they are being hindered;
through the land.

3.

1. Write out Pres. Indic. Middle of παύω.

2. Decline in Sing. with Article, ναύτης, ἀγορά,
δίψα.

3. 1st Sing. Imperf. Indic. Act. of ἀκούω, ἐλαύνω, εἰς-φέρω, ὁπλίζω.

4. Aorist Infin. and Participle Act. Middle and
Pass. of ποιέω.

5. Acc. and Dat. Sing. of ἱκανός, ἰσχυρός, ἄξιος.

6. What is meant by a "pure vowel"?   Give
examples.

7. Translate—Before the gates; the judge's
slaves; the men in the city; we heard the sailor;
he is hindered by the slave.

8. Translate—οἱ φεύγοντες. ἡσύχαζον ἐν τῇ
ἀγορᾷ. ἡσύχαζον οἱ ἐν τῇ ἀγορᾷ. σοφώτερός
ἐστι τοῦ κριτοῦ.

4.

1. Form the Future Indic. Act. of ἄγω, πέμπω, πείθω, ἐάω.

2. Write out Weak (or 1st) Aorist Indic. Act. and Middle of πλέκω.

3. Nom. and Gen. Sing. of κλεπτῶν, μαχῶν, τοξοτῶν, συμφορῶν.

4. Greek for—" he is," " they are," " he was," " they were ".

5. Write in small letters Ξ, Ρ, Γ, Λ, Δ, Η.

6. Parse ἐνομίζου, ὥρμησε, βοηθήσετε, κύκλῳ.

7. Correct οὐκ ὑμῖν, ἔπεμψε αὐτόν, ἐκ ἴσου, μετ' ἡμῶν.

8. Translate—After the battle; not only . . . but also; the gifts are beautiful; the men in the island are many.

5.

1. Form Imperf. Indic. Act. of προσπίπτω, ὑποφαίνω, ἐκβαίνω, ἀπάγω.

2. Write out Future Indic. Middle of παύω.

3. Parse ἐάσει, ἐψεύσατο, κατέχοι, ἐξεπέμφθη.

4. Give the Nom. and Gen. Sing. of μαθητάς, ναυμαχίᾳ, ὁπλίτῃ, θαλάττης.

5. Decline in Sing. βαθύς.

6. Give the derivation of Metropolis, Geography, Heptarchy, Microscope.

7. Write out the terminations of Perfect and Pluperf. Indic. Middle.

8. Translate—ὁ ἀγαθός ἐστι σοφός. ἀγαθός ἐστιν ὁ σοφός. οὐ πολλῷ ὕστερον. ἄνευ μάχης. μετὰ ταῦτα. μεθ' ὑμῶν.

6.

1. Form Aorist Indic. Act. of ὡρμάω, ἐκπέμπω, συναθροίζω, συγχωρέω.

2. Decline in Sing. with Article ἡμέρα, τράπεζα, δόλος.

3. Form Perfect Middle and Pass. of τρίβω, γράφω, πλέκω, ἀγγέλλω.

4. Decline in Plural βραχύς.

5. Acc. and Gen. Sing. of αὐτός, οὗτος, ὅδε.

6. Greek for—200, 50th, 9, 70, 1000, 8th.

7. Compound κατὰ + αἱρέω. σύν + λαμβάνω. ἐν + καλέω. ἀπὸ + ὁρμάω. ἐκ + ἄγω. πρὸ + ἔχω. περὶ + ὁράω.

8. Translate—Wise men are worthy of honour; we persuaded him; of this island; your father; these garments are beautiful.

7.

1. Write out Pres. Indic. Act. of νικάω, ἀσκέω.
2. Form Perf. Indic. Act. of ἀπορέω, πονέω, ζηλόω, φιλέω.
3. Parse ἤγετο, συνήθροισε, τετελεύτηκε, πέμψαντες.
4. Nom. Sing. and Pl. of μισθοῦ, ἱκετοῦ, δένδρου, σιγῆς, δεσποίνης.
5. Decline in Sing. ἰσχύς, ἕξις.
6. Name the Gutturals, Dentals, Labials, Nasals and Liquids.
7. Translate—διὰ ταῦτα. πρὸς τούτοις. οἱ νῦν. δίκαιοι οἱ θεοί. αὐτὸς ὁ στρατηγός. ὁ αὐτός στρατηγός. ὡς τάχιστα.
8. Translate—The sailors in the ships; after that battle; with these soldiers; hearing this they obeyed; do you not hear?

8.

1. Explain Temporal Augment. Give examples.
2. Write out Pres. Opt. Act. of διώκω, βούλομαι.
3. Decline in Plural τάξις, γονεύς.
4. Form Weak Aorist Indic. Pass. of ἀδικέω, πέμπω, ἀγγέλλω, ἀνάγω.
5. Write out Pres. and Imperf. Indic. of εἰμί.

6. Give the Nom. Sing., Gender and English of βίᾳ, δίκην, χρυσοῦ, ὁπλοῖς.

7. Dative Sing. and Plur. (all genders) of ἕκαστος, εὐρύς, μακρός.

8. Translate—He is wiser than you; in this city; I persuaded his father; we heard him speaking; what do you say?

9.

1. Form Imperf. Indic. Act. of ἐλλείπω, οἴομαι, ἐγκρούω, συλλαμβάνω.

2. Write out the terminations of Weak Future and Aorist Passive.

3. Give the Infinitives and Participles Active of νικάω.

4. Decline in Plural with Article ἄγγελος, ἔργον, πυλή.

5. Parse ἐβοήθουν, ὥρμησας, βούλει, ᾐτήσατο.

6. Nom. Sing. Gender and English of ἱερεῖς, μαθήσει, πεδίῳ, τείχεσι.

7. Translate—ὁ υἱὸς μείζων ἐστι τοῦ πατρός. κατὰ γῆν καὶ κατὰ θάλατταν. οἱ δὲ ταῦτα ἐποίησαν ὡς ἐκελευσεν.

8. Translate—Of that land; they ordered us not to do this; who are you? this great city; this city is great.

10.

1. Parse ὡρμίσαντο, παρῄνει, ἤχθοντο, κωλῦσαν, εὐπορῆσαι.

2. Decline in Sing. ποιητής, πεῖρα, γλῶσσα.

3. Reduplicate the following stems : βλαβ-, ῥιπ-, σκευαδ-, χωριδ-, αἱρε-, ψευδ-.

4. Imperf. Indic. of προσ-αιτέω, ἐγ-γράφω, συμ-βάλλω, ἡγέομαι, οἴχομαι.

5. Dative Sing. and Pl. of φανερός, βαρύς, δῆλος.

6. Greek for—16, 80, 300, 7th, 11th, 70th.

7. Translate—The slaves in the house are faithful ; the faithful slaves are in the house ; they were fleeing up that road ; we heard the judge himself.

8. Translate—οἱ φεύγοντες. οἱ πολῖται αὐτοί. οὗτοι οἱ πολῖται. τῇ ὑστεραίᾳ. ἐκ δὲ τούτου. διὰ ταῦτα.

11.

1. Form Fut. Indic. Act. of βλάπτω, φυλάσσω (or φυλάττω), σπεύδω, ἐάω.

2. Nom. Sing., Gender and English of ληστῶν, κινδύνων, εὐχῶν, ἀδελφῶν, τόξων.

3. Write out Pres. Imper. Act. and Middle of παύω.

4. Decline in Sing. ὀφρύς, ἄστυ.

5. Write out Perf. Indic. Pass. of πλέκω, γράφω.

6. Compare χαλεπός, κοῦφος, γλυκύς.

7. Contract τιμάου, δηλόομεν, δηλόῃ, τιμάῃς, φίλεε. Give the uncontracted forms of τιμῶο, φιλείσθω, τιμῶσα, ἐδήλου.

8. Translate—They were dying of disease : he. remained 3 days; of the king himself; in this island; those who were guarding the city.

12.

1. Write out Imperf. Indic. of νικάω, οἴχομαι.

2. Decline in Sing. θώραξ, ἅρμα.

3. Parse πειρώμενος, σώσασθαι, κελεύοι, ἐτέτακτο.

4. Decline in Sing. ἐγώ, in Plural σύ.

5. Form Weak Aorist Middle of ἄρχω, ἀποκομίζω, θεάομαι, πείθω.

6. Gen. Sing., Gender and English of νόσος, ὕπνος, μέρος.

7. Translate—τὰ πάλαι. διὰ τὸ τοὺς συμμάχους νενικῆσθαι. τί ἡμᾶς ἐξελαύνετε ; οἱ δὲ μετ᾽ αὐτοῦ ὄντες ἔφυγον.

8. Translate—In this manner; they hindered us by force; the guards are sleeping (καθεύδω) in

the market-place; the guards in the market-place are sleeping.

13.

1. Write out Pres. Indic. of ἡττάομαι, ἡγεόμαι.
2. Parse ἔσται, ἐστέ, ἦσαν, ἴθι.
3. Decline in Sing. σώφρων, ἀκρατής.
4. Give the Infins. and Participles Pass. of πείθω.
5. Nom. and Gen. Sing. of πατρίδας, ἱππέας, λιμένας, ἔπη.
6. Vocative Sing. of στρατηγός, γυνή, παῖς, ἀνήρ.
7. Translate—ἀγαθόν τι. τίνες δή εἰσιν οὗτοι; πάντων κράτιστος ἐνομίζετο. δεῖ ἡμᾶς μάχεσθαι.
8. Translate—By land and sea; we will send him; they were wronged (ἀδικέω) by him; you say the same things; this island is greater than that.

14.

1. Form Pres. Infin. Act. and Pass. of νικάω, ζημίοω, καλέω.
2. Decline in Sing. ἔτος, δῆμος.
3. Write out Fut. Indic. Act. and Middle of ἀγγέλλω.

4. Parse ᾤχοντο, ἔμειναν, ἦρξε, ἐνόμιζε, σωθέντες.

5. Derive Biography, Orthodox, Astronomy, Sympathy.

6. Acc. and Dat. Plural of τλήμων, παχύς, στενός.

7. Translate—πρὸς τούτοις. ἐκ τούτου. ἐν τούτῳ. πολλοί. οἱ πολλοί. τὸ πολύ. οἱ πλεῖστοι τῶν μετ' ἐκείνου.

8. Translate—We must do this; these things are true; they say that he is fleeing; the desire (ἐπιθυμία) of ruling; your mother.

15.

1. Form Imperf. Indic. of ἐγχώρεω, ἀξιόω, ἡγέομαι, αἰτέω.

2. Decline in Sing. νεότης, τεχνίτης.

3. Write out Aorist Act. and Middle of γράφω.

4. Give the Principal Tenses * of ἀπατάω, ἄρχω.

5. Decline in Plural ἀσφαλής, εὐδαίμων.

6. Distinguish Proper and Improper Diphthongs. Examples of each.

7. Give the Infinitives and Participles Pres. and Fut. of εἰμί.

* See "Explanatory," page vii.

8. Translate—τοὺς μὲν ἀπέκτειναν, τοὺς δὲ ζῶντας ἔλαβον. "οὐ γὰρ ἔστιν," ἔφη "χρήματα ἡμῖν." πῶς οὐ ταῦτα παντὶ τρόπῳ ἀδικώτερα ἐκείνων ;

9. Translate—We consider that those barbarians are friendly to us; send him to the city; do not send him; did you not send him? let us send him.

16.

1. Write out Pres. Indic. Act. of ζηλόω, θηράω.

2. Nom. and Gen. Sing. Gender and English of ἡδονῶν, τροπαίων, στομάτων, ἀνθῶν.

3. Fut. Indic. of ψεύδομαι, δράω, μένω, δέχομαι.

4. Parse ἠρώτα, ποιήσειε, ἐκοιμήθης, νικῶντας. ἰᾶσι.

5. Distinguish Weak (or 1st) and Strong (or 2nd) Aorist.

6. How is Time "when" and "within which" expressed? Give examples.

7. Write out Pres. and Aorist Indic. Act. of ἵστημι.

8. Translate—δρόμῳ ἐχώρει εἰς τὴν πόλιν. μὴ πείθεσθε τούτοις. ἡ ἐπιθυμία τοῦ πολλὰ ἔχειν. οὐκ ἔξεστί μοι ταῦτα ποιεῖν.

9. Translate—Day by day; the cities in that

island are many; in the middle of the road; those who heard this fled.

17.

1. Write out Imperf. Indic. Act. of βοηθέω, βοάω.

2. Decline in Plural ὄρος, ἱερεύς.

3. Form Perf. Indic. Act. of ἀγγέλλω, πείθω, ταράττω, γράφω.

4. Write out Pluperf. Middle and Pass. of κομίζω, φυλάττω.

5. Distinguish εἰμί, εἶμι. εἶναι, ἴεναι. ἦεσαν, ἦσαν. ἴσθι, ἴθι.

6. Acc. and Gen. Sing. of πολύς, μέγας, εὐρύς.

7. How are the Instrument and the Agent expressed in Greek?

8. Translate—οὐ χρημάτων ἕνεκα ἔπλευσαν. κελεῦσον ἀνοῖξαι τὰς πύλας. οὔκουν πορευσόμεθα; ἄπειμι ἵνα μὴ ἴδω.

9. Translate—In addition to this; on these conditions; our friends are more than our foes; all except one were saved; he says that this is true.

18.

1. Give the Infinitives and Participles Pass. of βλάπτω.

2. Write out Pres. Indic. Act. and Middle of ὁρμάω.

3. Parse ὡπλισμένοι, ζῶντας, ζημιοῦν, πέμψοιεν, ἔθηκε.

4. Gen. Sing. and Dat. Plural of φροντίς, δράκων, πάθος, χείμων.

5. Decline οὗτος in Singular.

6. Distinguish Strong and Weak Aorist Pass. Give examples of each.

7. Write out Imperf. Indic. Act. of δίδωμι.

8. Translate—αἱ αὐταί κῶμαι. αὗται αἱ κῶμαι. αἱ κῶμαι αὐταί. αὐταί κῶμαι. ἆρ᾽οὐ καλόν ἐστι ; διὰ τὶ θαυμάζετε;

9. Translate—According to this law ; contrary to the law ; up the road ; he spoke thus, and they replied as follows.

19.

1. Imperfect Indic. Act. of ἐλλείπω, παραινέω, ἔχω, αἰτιάομαι.

2. Write out Pres. Optat. Act. of νικάω.

3. Principal Tenses of τρίβω, φυλάττω.

4. Write out Imperf. Indic. of εἶμι (go) and ἵημι.

5. Decline in Sing. πλοῦς, κρατήρ.

6. Compare ταχύς, εὐδαιμών, ἀληθής, μέσος.

7. Vocative of Σοφοκλῆς, Ἑρμῆς, Πέρσης, πατήρ, γυνή.

8. Translate—It is not possible to do this; I sent your slave; will you not obey him? he is skilled (ἔμπειρος) in speaking.

9. Distinguish παρὰ σοῦ, παρὰ σοί, παρὰ σέ. πρός τινος, πρός τινι, πρός τι.   μετά τινος, μετά τι.

20.

1. Write out Pres. Indic. Act. and Mid. of ἵημι.

2. Decline in Sing. ἔτος, ναύτης.

3. Dative Sing. and Pl. of οὗτος, ταχύς, ἀληθής.

4. Pres. and Aor. Infin. Act. of τίθημι, ἵστημι, δίδωμι.

5. Give rules for Reduplication, with examples.

6. Parse ᾐτιῶντο, ἐνίκα, κατέλιπε, ἐνέκλιναν, ἔθεσαν.

7. Give Nom. and Gen. Sing., Gender and English of πρέσβεις, ἀπορίαν, ἀσπίδων, ἔχθρας, νύκτα.

8. Translate—ἐκέλευον θέσθαι τὰ ὅπλα. ἔδοσαν ἃ ᾔτουν. ἀπήλαυνον οἴκαδε. τῇ ἐπιούσῃ νυκτί.

9. Translate—They stood in the middle of the

road; your son is bigger than mine; I heard the
messenger himself saying this.

21.

1. Write out Pres. Indic. Act. of πλέω, ζάω.
2. Decline in Sing. ὄφις, δελφίς.
3. Form Aor. Act. of ἀναπηδάω, συναθροίζω, ἐπι-
κηρύττω, συμβάλλω.
4. Dat. Sing. and Pl. of ταχύς, ἀληθής, σώφρων.
5. Parse πράξῃς, βλέψον, ἠφανίσθη, ἠναγκάσ-
μεθα, μεθέστηκε.
6. Name and classify the Mutes and Semi-
vowels.
7. Imperf. and Strong Aor. Indic. Act. of ἵστημι, ἵημι, δίδωμι.
8. Translate—ἔφη βούλεσθαι ἐλθεῖν. ἔτυχε
μείζων ὤν. δῆλοι ἦσαν ἐλπίζοντες. ἠρώτων τί
χρὴ ποιεῖν.
9. Translate—You must not do this; did you
not hear him? the garments were beautiful; they
consult about the war.

22.

1. Write out Pres. Imperative Active of ποιέω,
σιγάω.

2. Nom. Sing. and Plur. of ἄνθεσι, τραύμασι, τάξεσι, θεράπουσι.

3. Pluperf. Indic. Act. of ζημιόω, νικάω, ἀπο-στερέω, προχωρέω.

4. Name five feminine words of 2nd Declension, with English.

5. Principal Tenses of πέμπω, ἀδικέω.

6. Write out the terminations of Strong Aorist Indicative Active and Middle.

7. Parse τιθέναι, ἵεντο, ἵστη, στῇ, δός.

8. Translate—αὕτη ἡ πόλις. ἡ πόλις αὕτη. ἡ αὐτή πόλις. αὐτὴ ἡ πόλις. ὁρῶ τοὺς ἐν τῇ ἀγορᾷ. ὁρῶ αὐτοὺς ἐν τῇ ἀγορᾷ.

9. Translate—He spoke on behalf of the generals; not long afterwards; they conquered their enemies; many were dying of hunger (λιμός).

23.

1. Show how the various Diphthongs are augmented.

2. Fut. Indic. Act. of ἀγγέλλω, κομίζω, κερδαίνω, καλύπτω, δίδωμι.

3. Write out Aorist Imper. Act. and Middle of παύω.

4. Perf. Middle and Pass. of διαθρύπτω, ἀπο-κηρύττω, ὁπλίζω, ἀφαιρέω.

5. Decline in Sing. τόλμα, πνεῦμα.

6. Gen. and Acc. Sing. of χρυσοῦς, ἄδικος, ἀκρι-βής.

7. What Greek Interrogative Particles corre-spond to the Latin Nonne and Num ?

8. Translate—Those who announced this vic-tory; the greater part of the country; we are fighting for our country.

9. Translate—οἱ Ἀθηναῖοι οὐκ ἐβοήθουν διὰ τὸ μὴ πυνθάνεσθαι τὴν πολιορκίαν. πάντων πάντα κράτιστος ἐνομίζετο.

24.

1. Write out Pres. Subj. Act. of ἀγαπάω, ζηλόω.

2. Gen. Sing., Gender and English of ὄρος, ὅρος, χίων, δράκων.

3. Form Weak Aorist Pass. of ἀθροίζω, κα-λύπτω, αἰσχύνομαι ἐλέγχω.

4. Name Six Verbs which take a Strong Aorist Active.

5. Decline in Plural οὗτος.

6. Principal Tenses of ἀνύτω, φυλάττω.

7. Greek for—15, 22, 500, 10,000, twice.

B

8. Translate—I did it myself: in the same house; those with him; according to this law; to receive from any one.

9. Translate—ἆρ᾽ οὐ δεῖ ἡμᾶς παύσασθαι τοῦδε τοῦ πολέμου; οἱ ναῦται ἐξ ἐνίων τῶν νεῶν ἄρτι ἐξέβαινον.

25.

1. Form Aorist Indic. Act. of μένω, σημαίνω, ἀπαγγέλλω, διαρπάζω, τίθημι.

2. Write out Imperf. Indic. of οἴομαι, ἀπαντάομαι.

3. Compare κακός, πολύς, καλός, μέγας.

4. Parse ἤρετο, ἠξίου, ἀποκτενοῦμεν, καθορᾷ, ὥρμηντο.

5. Form Nom. Sing. from the stems κτηματ-, αἰθερ-, ἱμαντ-, ἠθες-.

6. Write out Perf. Indic. Middle of πέμπω, ψεύδομαι.

7. How is "than" (Comparative) expressed in Greek?

8. Translate—They fled by night from that city: we must, therefore, hinder them by force; we ordered him not to go, but he did not obey.

9. Contract ζηλόητε, τιμάου, τιμάῃς, δηλόῃ,

δηλόει. Correct κατ᾽ ἡμέραν, τέτριβμαι, λεγθῆναι, δαίμονσι.

26.

1. Write out Pres. Optative of ἀξιόω, ἡγέομαι.

2. Strong Aorist Pass. of βλάπτω, σπείρω, ἐκπλήττω, σήπω.

3. Principal Tenses of ἅπτω, διώκω.

4. Decline in Sing. ὀξύς, ψευδής.

5. Parse ἴστη, ἔστη, τίθεσαι, ἀπιέναι, ἥσθη.

6. Nom. and Gen. Sing. of τριήρεσι, φάλαγγα, ἐλπίδων, ἱματίοις.

7. Decline the Reflexive Pronoun of the 1st Person.

8. Translate—πολλάκις τῆς ἡμέρας. λόγῳ γὰρ ἦσαν οὐκ ἔργῳ φίλοι. τὰ αὐτὰ λέγεις. αὐτῶν τῶν κριτῶν. ἐπείσω αὐτᾷ.

9. Translate—In addition to this; beyond (one's) power; contrary to the laws; they kill their own children; the walls of the city itself.

27.

1. Fut. Indic. of αἴρω, φράζω, ἰάομαι, κλέπτω, μένω.

2. Decline in Plural χείρ, βοῦς.

3. Infinitives and Participles Passive of πέμπω.

4. Acc. and Gen. Sing. and Plural of μέλας, τέρην, μείζων.

5. Parse ἐνίκα, ἐπύθοντο, ἐκπηδήσαντες, ἐᾶν.

6. Write out Pres. Indic. of αἰτιάομαι, φοβέομαι.

7. Decline αὐτόν.

8. Translate—ἐδόκει πέμψαι τὸν κήρυκα. ᾐσθό-μην αὐτόν Ἕλληνα ὄντα. οὐ πείθονται τοὺς ταῦτα λέγουσι.

9. Translate—Instead of obeying; in the middle of the city; when they heard what had happened (γίγνομαι) they went away.

28.

1. Write out Fut. Indic. Act. and Middle of σπείρω.

2. Nom. and Gen. Sing. of θηρία, ἀπορία, εἰρήνην, πρέσβεις.

3. Perf. Indic. Act. of βλάπτω, ἄρχω, ἁρπάζω, τάττω, ἵστημι.

4. Decline in Sing. ἀμείνων, τλήμων.

5. What verbs cannot (regularly) take a Strong Aorist Act. ?

6. Parse τιθῇ, ἰᾶσι, στῆναι, ἔδωκαν, ἀπεῖναι.

7. What is the ordinary construction after λέγω, φημί?

8. Distinguish μένει, μενεῖ. ἐσήμηνε, ἐσήμαινε. μέλει, μελλει. ὅρος, ὄρος. αὐτός, αὐτός. δουλοῖς, δούλοις.

9. He fled to his own house; they ordered us not to do this; they threw themselves into the sea: let some one lead the way (ἡγεόμαι).

29.

1. Pres. Infin. Act. and Pass. of ἀγαπάω, χειρόω, ἀποστερέω.

2. Dat. Sing. and Plural of δόλος, φονεύς, τέκτων, ἔπος.

3. Write out Aorist Indic. Act. and Middle of ἀγγέλλω.

4. Parse ἀποκτεῖναι, ᾤοντο, ἐδόκουν, θεῖεν, ἵστη.

5. Decline τίς.

6. How would you describe the letters δ, φ, κ, μ, σ, ρ?

7. Write out Aorist Indic. Act. and Middle of ἵημι.

8. Translate—πορεύεται ὡς βασιλέα ἱππέας ἔχων ὡς πεντακοσίους. ἀνέβη ἐπὶ τὰ ὄρη οὐδένος κωλύοντος. κατὰ φύσιν.

9. Translate—On that day; you must obey him: we use these weapons: they burn (κατα-καίω) the boats that he may not cross (διαβαίνω).

30.

1. Write out Pres. and Imperf. Indic. of τίθημι.
2. Decline in Sing. τέλος, φύσις, φονεύς.
3. Compare ἄξιος, τλήμων, σαφής, πολύς.
4. Parse ᾔδει, φῇ, ἰέναι, ἦσθα, ἔσει.
5. Distinguish αὐτόν, αὑτόν. ταῦτον, ταὐτόν. αὗται, αὐταί.
6. Acc. and Dat. Plural of δόλος, μέρος, αὐλητής, γυμνής, θεράπων, τέκτων.
7. Aorist Infin. and Participles (all voices) of φαίνω.
8. Translate—By force; by night; they were not so base as to flee; they were so base that they fled; he happened to be sleeping (καθεύδω).
9. Translate—ἐγίγνωσκεν ὅτι οἱ τριήραρχοι οἴκοι καθευδήσοιεν. δῆλοι ἦσαν προσελαύνοντες οἱ πολέμιοι.

31.

1. Imperf. Indic. Act. of προσαιτέω, προβαίνω, ἐγκλίνω.

2. What Verbs usually form Perf. Act. with -κα? what with -α?

3. Write out Imperative Subj. and Perf. Middle of πείθω.

4. Principal Tenses of λείπω, ῥίπτω.

5. Decline πῆχυς, and name words declined like it.

6. Parse κατέστην, ἀφίεται, ἔθεσαν, μεθῆκε, ἐδυνάμεθα.

7. Acc. Plural of the three Reflexive Pronouns.

8. Translate—Some were killed, others fled; let us cease fighting; do not give him these weapons; he hoped to do this.

9. Translate—διὰ ταῦτα, μετὰ ταῦτα, ἐν τούτῳ, πρὸς τούτοις. ἔστην, ἔστηκα, ἔστησα, στήσω. τὸ γεγενημένον.

32.

1. Point out peculiarities in Pres. Indic. of πλέω and ζάω.

2. Write out Aorist Subj. Act. and Middle of καλύπτω.

3. Aorist Indic. Act. of λείπω, λαμβάνω, θνήσκω, πίπτω, ἔρχομαι.

4. Write out Pluperf. Indic. Pass. of πείθω, γράφω.

5. Decline in Sing. ἔαρ, Ζεύς.

6. Compare νέος, ῥᾴδιος, μικρός, ἀγαθός.

7. What is the construction of Indirect Questions in Greek ?

8. Translate—οὐ δεῖ ἡμᾶς ταῦτα παθεῖν ὑφ' ὑμῶν. ἐτάχθησαν ἐπὶ τεττάρων. οἱ ἐκ τῆς ἀγορᾶς ἔφυγον.

9. Translate—This will be more useful to you than to us; instead of going up the country, he sailed away.

33.

1. Fut. Indic. Act. of σπείρω, ἀλείφω, τρέφω, θηράω, ἀφίημι.

2. Write out Strong Aorist Subj. of λείπω, πείθομαι.

3. Point out peculiarities in the declension of μήτηρ, ἀνήρ, ὕδωρ.

4. Parse δοίη, ἵστασαν, εἷσαν, ἐπέβη, τιθεῖο.

5. Decline in Plural μείζων, πλήρης.

6. What is the construction of a Final Clause ?

7. Parse ὁρῶσα, μετιόντας, ἐμβαλούσης.

8. Translate—ἐκ τοῦ ἴσου μαχοῦνται. ἅμα τῇ ἡμέρᾳ. μέγιστον τῶν κακῶν τυγχάνει ὂν τὸ ἀδικεῖν.

9. Translate—The war against the Persians; they were marching through the land; they took the triremes, crews and all.

34.

1. Perf. Indic. Middle of ἅπτω, καταψηφίζω ἀκούω, ἀποκηρύττω.

2. Gen. and Dat. Sing. of θρασύς, σιδήρους, ἵλεως.

3. Write out Pres. Imperat. of ἡγέομαι, ὁρμάομαι, ἵσταμαι.

4. Parse ἐβόα, λίπωμαι, πεμφθῇς, πέπεισαι, εἶναι.

5. Nom. Sing., Gen. and English of θῆρας, κύνες, ὠτός, λαμπάδας.

6. Aorist Indic. Middle of αἰτέω, ψηφίζομαι, ἀφίημι, λαμβάνω.

7. How is a Negative Command expressed in Greek?

8. Translate—εὖ ἐπάθομεν ὑπ' αὐτῶν. ὑμεῖς οὖν νομίζετε σοφοὶ εἶναι. ἐπλήρουν τάς ναῦς ὡς ἀναξόμενοι.

9. Translate—When this happened, we fled;

you must send a herald; he came with 500 hoplites; he said he was not willing.

35.

1. Write out Aor. Opt. Act. and Mid. of τιμάω.
2. Accus. Plur. of αὐτός, αὑτός, οὗτος, αὐτόν.
3. Weak Aor. Indic. Pass. of ἁναρπάζω, ἅπτω, ἄρχω, ἁκούω, τίθημι.
4. Gen. and Accus. Sing. of ἅρμα, ἧττα, λαμπρότης, νομοθέτης.
5. Compare ὀλίγος, ἡδύς, αἰσχρός, ἄφθονος.
6. Infinitives and Participles Act. of στέλλω.
7. Derive Epitaph, Syntax, Hydrophobia, Sympathy.
8. Translate—He ordered his own horsemen to follow; they were dying of famine; we consider that he is wise; until evening.
9. Translate—αἰσχύνομαι λέγων. αἰσχύνομαι λέγειν. ἆρα μὴ ἔπεμψας; ἆρ' οὐκ ἔπεμψας; πᾶσα πόλις. πᾶσα ἡ πόλις.

36.

1. Perf. Indic. Act. of στέλλω, κλέπτω, πέμπω, ῥίπτω.
2. Write out Pres. Opt. Act. of ὁράω, δοκέω.

3. Decline in Sing. γάλα, γυνή.

4. Parse ἐτίμω, ἐποιήσω, ἀπαγγεῖλαι, σπεροῦμεν.

5. Decline in Plural ὅστις.

6. Distinguish the meanings Active and Middle of αἱρέω, παύω, πορίζω, τιμωρέω.

7. Nom. and Gen. Sing. of εὔφροσι, εὐθεῖαν, εὐσεβεῖς, χαρίεσι.

8. Translate—σοφός ὁ κριτής. αὐτός ταῦτα γέγραφα. ἠπόρουν τί χρὴ ποιεῖν. οὐ πείθονται τοῖς ταῦτα λέγουσι.

9. Translate—He says that these things are true; he said that these things were true; he commanded the swiftest of the ships to follow them.

37.

1. Principal Tenses of σπεύδω, σπείρω.

2. Nom. Sing., Gender and English of τείχεσι, ὄφεσι, θέρους, λίθους.

3. Imperf. Indic. of ῥίπτω, καθαιρέω, δυστυχέω, ἕπομαι.

4. Parse ᾖεσαν, ἀφεῖσαν, θές, ἔστησε, παρήλασε.

5. Explain θάτερα, τἀνδρί, χἠ, ἐγῷμαι, κἀγω, κᾆτα.

6. Write out Aorist Indic. Middle of ψεύδομαι, τίθημι.

7. Give an example of Genitive Absolute.

8. Translate—He himself was slain, but those with him fled; all came except one ; come to the ships that we may sail; she has small hands.

9. Distinguish ἤ, ἥ, ἦ, ᾖ, ᾗ.   Contract τιμάοιο, τιμάουσα, φιλέεσθε, δηλόῃ, ὀστέα, εὐγένεα, χρυσέαν, ἀργυρέᾳ.

38.

1. Write out Pres. Indic. Act. of ἰάομαι, μεθίημι.

2. Nom. Sing., Gender and English of ἄλγει, δυνάμει, γονεῖ, κρέᾳ, υἱεῖ.

3. Future Indic. Middle of πειράω, νομίζω, φθείρω, καλέω.

4. Parse νικῴη, βούλησθε, ὤκνει, ᾐτήσατο, εἰδέναι.

5. Acc. Sing. and Dat. Pl. of λαβών, πεφευγώς, ζῶν, πεμφθείς.

6. How are Consecutive Clauses constructed ?

7. Distinguish αὐτή, αὑτή, αὕτη.   ἐκεῖ, ἐκεῖσε, ἐκεῖθεν.   ἀπεῖναι, ἀπιέναι, ἀφιέναι.

8. Translate—Tell me who you are ; hearing this he was silent ; must we not obey the laws ? nothing is more disgraceful than flight.

9. Translate—τούτοις τοῖς ἡγέμοσι ἐχρῶντο. τούτοις ἡγέμοσι ἐχρῶντο.   τίνα πέμψομεν ; τίνα πέμψωμεν ;

39.

1. Write out Pres. Subj. of τελευτάω and φοβέομαι.

2. Aorist Indic. Act. of πίπτω, λανθάνω, βαίνω, γιγνώσκω, φέρω.

3. Which form of the Perfect Active is usual in Guttural, Dental, Labial, and Nasal Verbs?

4. Compare λάλος, μέσος, ἀγαθός, πολύς.

5. Decline in Plural χείρ, πούς, ναῦς.

6. Name words declined (1) like μήτηρ, (2) like πῆχυς.

7. Parse σωθῇ, ἔσοιτο, εἰδυῖα, ἀφίεντες.

8. Translate—He said (ἔφη) he was a Persian, but we perceived that he was a Greek; instead of pursuing, they are themselves pursued.

9. Translate—ἅμα τῷ ἡλίῳ δύνοντι. τῇ ἐπιούσῃ νυκτί. ἑλοίμην ἂν μᾶλλον ἀδικεῖσθαι ἢ ἀδικεῖν.

40.

1. Parse καταβάντι, σιωπήσειε, ἡγῇ, γενοῦ, ἑάλω.

2. Gen. Sing. and Dat. Plural of μάντις, στάχυς, σκεῦος, χειμών.

3. Principal Tenses of τίθημι, δίδωμι.

4. Decline in Sing. βαρύς, in Plural ψευδής.

5. Give the Greek Pronouns corresponding to ille, ipse, quis? se, eum.

6. Distinguish ἄλλος, ἕτερος. μέλει, μέλλει. ἔστη, ἔστησε.

7. Give rules for Reduplication, with examples.

8. Translate—οἱ δὲ Λακεδαιμόνιοι οὐκ ἔφασαν σπείσεσθαι. σπονδῶν ἐπὶ τούτοις γενομένων. μετεπέμπετο χρήματα Ἀθήνηθεν.

9. Translate—They said that the river was wide; we came that we might hear you; are they slaves or free men?

41.

1. Write out Fut. Indic. Act. and Middle of βάλλω.

2. Decline in Sing. υἱός, ὄρνις.

3. Weak Aorist Indic. Act. of ἐγκλίνω, προτείνω, ὀνειδίζω, διαλλάττω, ἀφίημι.

4. Nom. and Acc. Sing. of πλήρεις, οἰκείας, ἐλάττους, μεγάλην.

5. Parse ἐσήμηνε, ἤρξαντο, τέθνηκε, εἰδότες, ἀπίουσι.

6. Principal Tenses of αἴρω, ἄρχω.

7. Which Negative is used in Direct Questions?

8. Derive τρόπος, γένεσις, πνεῦμα, σωτήρ, ζω-γρέω. Distinguish πόλεμέω, πολεμοω. δουλόω, δουλεύω. ὡρμάω, ὁρμέω.

9. Translate—Many of the fugitives were slain by the horsemen; it being summer (θέρος) all the roads were deserted (ἔρημος).

42.

1. Pluperf. Indic. Pass. of ἀπογράφω, παρα-σκευάζω, θύω, οἰκοδομέω.

2. Give rules for the Augment of Compound Verbs.

3. Gen., Gender and English of θησαυρός, γνά-θος, πλῆθος, τραῦμα.

4. Parse ἐδόθη, τέθειμαι, δοῦναι, ἵστασο, ἠπί-στατο.

5. Write out Aorist Imperat. Act. of βλέπω, and Middle of σκέπτομαι.

6. Derive Phosphorus, Kilogramme, Schism, Cataract, Caustic.

7. What is the construction of an Indirect Negative Command? Give examples.

8. Translate—My brother having died, they would not remain; the cause of the present war; they are much stronger than we (are).

9. Translate with Notes—ἔφασαν προδώσειν τὴν πόλιν. οὐδεὶς τούτων ὧν ὁρῶ. ὁ δὲ εἶπεν ὅτι καλῶς ἔχοι ἀποπλεῦσαι.

43.

1. Perf. Indic. Act. of λείπω, σπείρω, τρέφω, θνήσκω, ἵστημι.

2. Decline in Plural ἀκούσας, πεφευγώς.

3. Parse κομιεῖν, ἐψεύσω, ἀπώλοντο, ἔγνω, οἰκιοῖτο.

4. Infinitives and Participles Active of φθείρω.

5. In what Stems (3rd Declension) is σ rejected in the Nominative?

6. Distinguish αὗται, αὐταί, αὑταί, αὐτούς.

7. Explain (with examples) Definite and Indefinite Relative Clauses.

8. Translate—It is evident that they are friendly; he said he was a Greek; they said that many died; he went to his own city.

9. Translate—κατὰ κράτος. ἐν τῷ παρόντι. τῷ ὄντι. μὰ τοὺς θεούς. ἐξ ἀπροσδοκήτου. δι᾽ ὀλίγου. ὑπὸ νύκτα.

44.

1. Principal Tenses of εὑρίσκω, καλέω.

2. Name Feminine words in -ος, 2nd Decl.

3. Imperf. Indic. Act. of ἕρπω, ὁράω, καθεύδω, αὐξάνω.

4. Write out Weak Aor. Opt. and Imperat. Act. of πείθω.

5. Decline in Sing. τάλας, εὐρύς.

6. Distinguish ἴθι, ἴσθι. εἴη, ᾔει. ἰέναι, ἰέναι. ἰῇ, ἴῃ. ἰστάναι, ἐστάναι.

7. Show the construction of Consecutive Clauses.

8. Translate—They therefore persuaded him in this way; he asked what we wanted; they went down the road (leading) to the sea.

9. Distinguish the Active and Middle meanings of ἄρχω, αἱρέω, βουλεύω, διδάσκω, λαμβάνω.

45.

1. Write out Pres. Indic. of φοβέομαι, αἰτιάομαι.

2. Decline Sing. and Plur. of πούς, οὖς.

3. Write out Perf. Indic. Pass. of βλάπτω, φράζω.

4. Parse ᾔσθετο, δυνήσει, ἠγγέλθη, ἡμάρτηκας, ἀφήσει.

5. Compare πίων, ὄψιος, παλαιός, ἄξιος, κακός.

6. Aorist Indic. Pass. of κοιμάω, αἰσχύνομαι, φθείρω, κρίνω.

C

7. How is a Wish referring to Future Time expressed? Example.

8. Translate—When they heard this they were amazed (ἐκπλήττω); they perceived that the messengers had come.

9. Translate—οὐκ ἐψεύσθη τῆς ἐλπιδος. οὐκ ἥκιστα τούτου ἕνεκα τὰς γυναῖκας ἀπέπεμψα. ἡ μέση πολις. μέση ἡ πόλις.

46.

1. Write out Pres. Imperat. of οἴομαι, σιγάω.

2. Future Indic. of κερδαίνω, σπένδω, οἰκίζομαι, λαμβάνω, πίπτω.

3. Parse ἄστει, ἐξέτασιν, φρουροὺς, πυροῖς, ὦτα.

4. Form and compare Adverbs from σοφός, ταχύς, εὐμενής, ἡδύς.

5. Aorist Infinitive and Participle (all Voices) of τρέπω.

6. English of ἔστη, ἔστησε, ἕστηκε, ἔστω, ᾔδεσαν.

7. Explain the various uses of αὐτός.

8. Translate—He happened to be writing; what did you say? we are not so foolish (ἀνόητος) as to trust this man.

9. Translate—ἀλγεῖ τὴν κεφαλήν. οὐκ οἷός τ᾽ ἦν κατέχειν τὰ δάκρυα. τοῦ ἐπιγιγνομένου θέρους. ἐπιγιγνομένου τοῦ θέρους.

47.

1. Write out Pres. Opt. Act. of πλέω, νικάω.

2. Parse ἀνήχθησαν, ἐπιστείλας, ἔασον, ἠρώτα, εἶεν.

3. Nom. Sing., Gender and English of γρᾶες, ὕδατι, ὄρει, χιόνι.

4. Aor. Indic. Act. of βοάω, πλέω, καλέω, εὑρίσκω, τίθημι.

5. Explain Elision, Crasis. Give examples.

6. Acc. Sing. and Pl. of τιμῶν, δηλῶν, ἐκβεβηκώς.

7. Give the Accus. Plur. of the three Reflexive Pronouns.

8. Translate—As quickly as possible; both by sea and by land; they said that (ὅτι) they would send three waggons; do not say that.

9. Translate—ἔπεμψεν ὡς Περδίκκαν πρέσβεις. εἰς καιρὸν ἥκεις. ᾑρέθη πρεσβευτὴς δέκατος αὐτός. τό γε εἶδος ὅμοιος εἶ τούτοις.

48.

1. Aorist Indic. of γίγνομαι, πάσχω, ἀποθνήσκω, αἰνέω, ἔχω.

2. Parse φύσει, πελέκει, ἄστη, νεώ, ἦρος.

3. Write out Imperf. Indic. of εἶμι and εἰμί.

4. Vocative Sing. of ἄναξ, παῖς, γυνή, κύων.

5. Parse συνέθεντο, ἀπέδοσαν, ἐπίθηται, ἀφεῖναι.

6. When is οὐ used in Relative Clauses? when μή?

7. Principal Tenses of ἔρχομαι, αἱρέω.

8. Translate—Let us sacrifice; whom are we to send? I know he is living; I bid you do this that you may get (λαμβάνω) some food.

9. Translate—πολεμικῶς ὑμῖν εἶχον. πρὶν τὰ νῦν πεπραγμένα γενέσθαι. μὴ τοσόνδ᾽ ἔλθοι κακόν. ὁ καθ᾽ ἡμέραν βίος.

49.

1. Explain "Strong Perfect". In what verbs is it usually found?

2. Parse ἠπόρουν, ἐχρῆτο, θαρσυνεῖ, ἀπῆραν, ἤρετο.

3. Nom. and Gen. Sing. of αὐτονόμους, ἅπαντα, ἐναντία, ὄντας.

4. Write out Pres. Subj. of ἀξιόω, νικάω.

5. Derive Planet, Catholic, Horizon, Pentecost, Pedagogue.

6. Decline ναῦς, γραῦς.

7. Explain the construction "Nominative and Infinitive". Give example.

8. Translate—εὖ πράττειν. χαλεπῶς φέρειν.

˙τί φῶ; τῷ ἐπίοντι ἔτει. πρὸς ταῦτα. ἐν τούτῳ. ἐκ τούτου.

9. Translate — It was announced that the enemy had been defeated; if you follow me, I will lead you to the city.

50.

1. Parse συλληφθῆναι, ἄγου, διηρώτων, ἀφέντες.

2. Write out Perf. Pass. of κλέπτω, ἁρπάζω.

3. Gen. Sing. and Dat. Plural of ἄκανθα, κῦμα, δεσπότης, ἐσθής.

4. Decline in Plural μείζων, ἀληθής.

5. Perf. Indic. Act. of εὑρίσκω, βαίνω, καλέω, στέλλω.

6. Point out peculiarities in Declension of χαρίεις, παῖς, πούς, ἧπαρ.

7. Classify the Consonants.

8. Translate—Many fled, fearing they would be put to death; they themselves say they are hostile to no man.

9. Translate—περὶ πολλοῦ ποιεῖσθαι. βουλοίμην ἂν τοῦτο γενέσθαι. τοὺς ἐνταῦθα πεσόντας ὑποσπόνδους ἀπεδίδου.

51.

1. Perf. Indic. Pass. of φθείρω, καίω, τελέω, στρέφω.

2. Decline ἑαυτόν.

3. Fut. Indic. Act. of καλέω, κρίνω, ἔχω, βάλλω, νομίζω.

4. Nom. Sing., Gender and English of ἅλας, μῆρας, γέρουσι, κόρακες.

5. Write out Imperf. Indic. Act. of ζάω, πλέω.

6. Distinguish εἰ, εἶ. ἦν, ἦν, ἦν. εἷς, εἰς.

7. Give rule for forming Weak Aorist Act. of Nasal and Liquid Verbs.

8. Translate—He announced that (ὅτι) these things were true; not in word only, but also in deed; at daybreak.

9. Translate—δίκην διδόναι. ἐν τῷ λοιπῷ χρόνῳ. ἔστιν ὅτε. πολλοί. οἱ πολλοί. οὐκ οἷός τ᾽ εἰμι ταῦτα ποιεῖν.

52.

1. Write out Pres. Indic. of χράομαι, θέω.

2. Positive and Comparative of ῥᾷστος, ἄριστος, ἔχθιστος, μακάρτατος.

3. Perf. Indic. Act. of θαυμάζω, ῥίπτω, ἐθέλω, γιγνώσκω, πίπτω.

4. Derive δεσμός, ῥήτωρ, γονεύς, πομπή, λήθη.

5. Parse προὔθηκε, ἀπεκρίνατο, ἠγωνίσω, σκέψασθε.

6. Principal Tenses of λαμβάνω, φαίνω.

7. Distinguish ἔλεγον τοιάδε. τοιαῦτα εἶπον. ἐάν, ἐᾶν. τὸ τροπαῖον ἕστηκε. τροπαῖον ἔστησε.

8. Translate—We escaped unobserved; they perceived that we had arms; we will cease fighting; may you be happy.

9. Translate—δῆλοι ἦσαν ἀποροῦντες. εἴθε μὴ ἐγένετο. ἔλεγον ὅτι δίκαιος εἴη ζημιοῦσθαι.

53.

1. Fut. Indic. Pass. of ῥίπτω, ταράττω, πείθω, κρίνω, ἀκούω.

2. Parse ἐστῶτος, δοθήσεται, ὑπέστη, φήσει, ἀφεῖμαι.

3. Gen. Sing., Gender and English of χειμών, γείτων, μαθητής, ταχυτής, τόλμα, μνῆμα.

4. Aorist Infin. Act. of εὐπορέω, ἀπαγγέλλω, διδάσκω, καλέω, ἀφίστημι.

5. Write out Pres. Subj. Act. of ζάω, ζημιόω.

6. Acc. Sing. and Dat. Plural of νενικηκώς, ὁρῶν, κρίνας, διδούς.

7. Explain the form of γένους, τέθνηκα, θρίξ, σπείσομαι.

8. Translate—It was not yet reported that they were dead; obey my words, if I seem to you to speak the truth.

9. Translate—πότερος ὑμῶν πρεσβύτερος ; μῶν μή τι ἠδίκηκας τὸν πατέρα ; δίκαιός εἰμι εἰπεῖν.

54.

1. Write out Fut. Indic. Act. of τελέω, πελάζω.

2. Nom. Sing., Gender and English of ἥπατος, ἀηδοῦς, ἕω, κράτει.

3. Parse πείθου, λάβῃ, δέχεσθαι, βοῶσαι, ᾔδεσαν.

4. Perf. Indic. Pass. of βάλλω, γιγνώσκω, καίω, λαμβάνω, δείκνυμι.

5. English of ἄλλοθι, ἄλλοσε, ἄλλοθεν, ποῖος, πόσος, ποῦ.

6. Which Tenses in each Voice admit of Strong forms ? Give example of each.

7. Compare ταχέως, μάλα, ἄνω.

8. Translate—Instead of pursuing our enemies, we are ourselves pursued; you will die dishonoured (δυσκλεής) when you die.

9. Translate—ἀπράκτους ἀπέπεμψεν. κατὰ τὸ δυνατόν. ἄλλοι ἄλλῃ τῆς πόλεως ἀπώλλυντο, ἔνιοι ἀνέπαυοντο,

55.

1. Principal Tenses of τρέπω, θάπτω.
2. Write out Imperf. Indic. of αἰτιάομαι, αἰτέω.
3. Give the Nom. Sing. (all Genders) of the Demonstrative and Definitive Pronouns.
4. Fut. Indic. of πίπτω, βούλομαι, μάχομαι, γίγνομαι, γιγνώσκω.
5. Nom. Sing., Gender and English of φρένας, ψυχάς, γεφύρας, ἱμάντας.
6. Write out Perf. Act. of ἵστημι.
7. What uses of Gen. and Dat. in Greek correspond to Latin Ablative?
8. Translate—οἵ τε ἄλλοι σύμμαχοι καὶ οἱ Αθηναῖοι. ἐπίστευον μὴ ἠδικηκέναι. ἤρωτα ἐπὶ τίσιν ἂν σύμμαχος γένοιτο.
9. Translate—He said they were slaves, but that he was a free (man); they were slain by the Greeks; he has a large head; he said this was true.

56.

1. Aorist Indic. of μάχομαι, καθαίρω, ἐλαύνω, ἀπαίρω, καθίστημι.
2. Decline κλείς, κύων.

3. Parse γεγενῆσθαι, ἤτουν, ἔφασαν, μεθεῖτο, ἑστῶτος.

4. Explain Coronis, Diaeresis, Paragogic ν.

5. Write out Perf. Pass. of πλέκω, γράφω.

6. Give the meanings of, and cases governed by, ὑπό, διά, παρά.

7. Acc. and Gen. Sing. of οὐδείς, θάσσων, μέγας, ἁπλοῦς.

8. Translate—They persuaded him to give them a garrison (φρουροί, Plural): when this happens we will lead the way (ἡγέομαι); on these terms.

9. Translate—οἱ μὲν ὕπνον ἡροῦντο κατὰ μέρος, οἱ δὲ ἤλαυνον. ἀλλ᾽ ἴθι, ἔφη, πιθοῦ καὶ μὴ ἄλλως ποίει.

57.

1. Write out the terminations of Weak Aorist Opt. Act. and Pass.

2. Decline in Sing. οὗτος.

3. Parse διήλλαξαν, εἴργασται, ἤρετο, μαχούμεθα.

4. Compare πένης, αἰσχρός, ἀγαθός, κλέπτης.

5. Aorist Indic. of βλώσκω, αἱρέω, αἰσθάνομαι, ὄλλυμι, καθίημι.

6. Dat. Sing. and Plural of στάχυς, πρέσβυς, ὀφθαλμός, ἔθνος, χείρ.

7. How is a Negative Command expressed? Give examples.

8. Translate—προυεῖπον δὲ ταῦτα τοῦ μὴ λύειν ἕνεκα τὰς σπονδάς. δι' ὀλίγου. ἐξ ἴσου. παρὰ δόξαν. τῷ ὄντι.

9. Translate—Do you not hear? do cease talking; he spoke as follows; he said that to flee was disgraceful; you will fight whenever you wish.

58.

1. Write out Pres. Indic. Act. of βοάω, πεινάω.

2. Decline Sing. of ἄκανθα, μοῖρα, κῦμα.

3. Perf. Indic. Act. of εὑρίσκω, αἱρέω, ὁράω, θνήσκω, κατανοέω.

4. Principal Tenses of στέλλω, πράττω.

5. Explain Syncope, Crasis, Elision.

6. Parse ἠπιστήθη, καθήσομεν, ἀφῆκας, καθελεῖν, εἴασε.

7. Distinguish οἱ οὐ ποιοῦντες. οἱ μὴ ποιοῦντες.

8. Translate—οὐκ ἔστι τοὺς θανόντας ἐς φάος μολεῖν. ἡμῖν οὐδέν ἐστιν ἀγαθὸν εἰ μὴ ὅπλα καὶ ἀρετή.

9. Translate—We are in doubt (ἀπορέω) what to do; he did this that he might not be injured; if you wish to sail we do not hinder you.

59.

1. Strong Aorist Indic. Pass. of τρέφω, δείρω, ῥήγνυμι, φαίνω, θάπτω.

2. Gen. Sing., Gender and English of δρόσος, μῦθος, κέρδος, ἔτος.

3. Parse ἐπήνεσας, ἔφηναν, ἀπέβη, ἀκούσει, ἀφεῖσαν.

4. Write out Imperf. Indic. Act. of ἵστημι, τίθημι.

5. Decline Sing. of ἁπλοῦς, ἥσυχος.

6. Distinguish ἄλλα, ἀλλά. εἶπε, εἰπέ. νῦν, νυν. εἰ, εἶ. ἤ, ῆ.

7. Name three Verbs followed by Genitive, three by Dative.

8. Translate—φύγοιεν ἂν εἴ τις διώκοι. ἔφυγον ἂν εἴ τις ἐδίωξε. ἀπώλοντο νῆες πέντε αὐτοῖς ἀνδρασι.

9. Translate—It was announced that (ὅτι) the Greeks were victorious (νικάω); we wish to live for the sake of the children, that we may educate them.

60.

1. Parse ἐωθοῦντο, ἐφοίτα, μεθέξετε, ἀπῆραν, ἠγωνίσω.

2. Decline in Sing. κρέας, in Plur. υἱός.

3. Compare δόκιμος, ἡσυχαῖος, εὔνους, ἴσος.

4. Distinguish ἀπεῖναι, ἀφεῖναι. ἀπιέναι, ἀφιέναι.

5. Classify the uses of αὐτός.

6. Give the Infinitives of all Tenses of ἄρχω.

7. What is the construction of an Indirect Statement?

8. Translate—They asked whither we were sailing; if you go we will follow; do not leave my children; he gave me this himself.

9. Translate—μέχρις ἂν ἥκω αἱ σπονδαὶ μενόντων. οἱ πολέμιοι, οὓς ᾤοντο ἀποφυγεῖν, παρῆσαν.

61.

1. Write out Pres. Opt. of ἀξιόω, θεάομαι.

2. Decline in Sing. μάρτυς, κόρυς, ἔαρ.

3. Parse ἐβάλου, ποιείσθω, σπεῖραι, ἀγγείλω, ἀφίοιεν.

4. Perf. Indic. Pass. of ῥίπτω, στρέφω, φαίνω, νομίζω, ἐλαύνω.

5. Explain "Compensatory Lengthening". Give examples.

6. Give all Participles of τίθημι.

7. In what clauses is the Subjunctive used?

8. Translate—χαλεπῶς ἤνεγκεν. δέκα ἔτη βασιλεύει. μὴ γένοιτο. ἐπ᾽ ἀκροῦ τοῦ ὄρους. ἔνιοι. οἷός τ᾽ εἰμι.

9. Translate—I know you are worthy; what are we to do? they were fighting that they might not be enslaved.

62.

1. Imperf. Indic. Act. of ὠθέω, ἕλκω, ἐάω, ὁράω.

2. Principal Tenses of κλέπτω, νομίζω.

3. Nom. Sing., Gender and English of σίτου, ὅρκους, σπονδάς, τείχους.

4. Infinitives and Participles of θνήσκω.

5. Derive Apostle, Thermometer, Electricity, Cathedral, Crystal.

6. Write out Aorist Act. and Middle of τίθημι.

7. What corresponds to the Latin Gerund and Gerundive?

8. Translate—If we had not fled, we should have conquered; they said they would send a herald; they set up a trophy.

9. Translate—βουλόμενοι ἐς χεῖρας ἐλθεῖν. μὴ δῆτα δράσῃς ταῦτα. ὁρῶντες πολλὰς τὰς πολεμίας ναῦς.

63.

1. Write out Pluperf. Indic. Pass. of ἁρπάζω, στέλλω.

2. Decline in Plural οὗτος, ὅστις.

3. Parse πέμφθητι, ἦρτο, τιμῷης, ἔα, ἐτράπησαν.

4. Compare δικαίως, κακῶς, ἄνω, μάλα.

5. Future Indic. of ἐλαύνω, βαίνω, βοάω, φέρω, εὑρίσκω.

6. Principal Tenses of τελέω, λείπω.

7. Greek for·—uter? quantus? quo? talis, ibi, inde.

8. Translate—ἀθύμως εἶχον. ἔλαθον φεύγοντες. τί λέγωμεν; δῆλος εἶ ἀδικῶν. νοσῶν ᾔσθετο. μὰ τοὺς θεούς.

9. Translate—The next day they happened to be in that city; the river Euphrates; I fear he may come; I fear he may not come.

64.

1. Write out Future Indic. of κομίζω, βιβάζω.

2. Name six Feminine words of 2nd Decl. in -ος.

3. Parse ἔθου, ὑπέστην, ἑστᾶσι, ἀφιέναι, θῶμεν.

4. Principal Tenses of βάλλω, γίγνομαι.

5. Nom. and Gen. Sing. of μέλη, φρενί, οἰκέταις, λέχει, ἑστίας.

6. Participles and Infinitives Act. of λαμβάνω.

7. Decline in Plural ἀσθενής, πλείων.

8. Translate (with Notes)—ἤρετο τί ποιῶν μάλιστα ἂν χαρίζοιτο αὐτῷ. ἄλλο στράτευμα πρὸς ὦ εἶχε μετεπέμπετο.

9. Translate—If this is true, I am ready to send him ; they will do this in order to get money; he was chosen general with two others.

65.

1. Aorist Indic. of παρασκεύαζω, θερμαίνω, ψεύδομαι, ῥίπτω.

2. Decline in Sing. ὅστις, αὐτόν.

3. Parse ἐξεπλάγησαν, ἀπεχθήσει, ἤρετο, ἤρετο, ἀπώλεσας.

4. Decline ἀνήρ, βοῦς.

5. Write out Pres. Indic. Act. and Pass. of ζημιόω.

6. Acc. Sing. and Dat. Plur. of ἐξαχθείς, διδούς, ὁρῶν, εἰδώς.

7. Name the Prepositions governing two cases. Give meanings.

8. Translate—ταῦτα ἐγένετο. ταῦτα ἐγένετο ἄν. οὐκ ἂν πείσαις ποτέ. εἰς τοσοῦτον ἦλθον κινδύνου.

9. Translate—Whoever is willing to fight, let

GREEK GRAMMAR PAPERS. 49

us arm him; do not trust those citizens; he slew his own son for the sake of money.

66.

1. Write out Imperf. Indic. of ἀξιόομαι, θεάομαι.

2. Voc. Sing. of Ἕλλην, Ἡρακλῆς, Κριτίας, Ἀγησίλαος.

3. Pluperf. Indic. Pass. of διαιρέω, ὁπλίζω, λαμβάνω, τείνω, τίθημι.

4. Greek for—The same, whoever, whither? each other, which of the two?

5. Accent ὁρμηθεις, λαβουσα, νικωντας, φανηναι, αινεσαι.

6. Parse βελτίω, πιθοῦ, πένθους, προδούς, ἐσθῆτι.

7. Principal Tenses of λαμβάνω, τέμνω.

8. Translate—They bade him remain in the same place, but he did not obey them; do you not see that they are much more (numerous) than we?

9. Translate (with Notes)—ἦλθον ξὺν ὥπερ εἶχον οἰκετῶν πιστῷ μόνῳ. ἐκέλευον αὐτὸν λαβεῖν ὅντινα βούλοιτο.

67.

1. Aorist Indic. Pass. of εὑρίσκω, καλέω, τείνω, ἀναγκάζω, δίδωμι.

D

2. Decline in Plural θάττων, εὔνους.

3. Write out Pres. Subj. of ἀπορέω, ἰάομαι.

4. Parse εἰδέναι, σιωπήσειε, ἐφοίτα, ἤρθη, δέχει.

5. Decline in Sing. λαγώς, ἥρως.

6. Distinguish the meanings of Present and Aorist Infinitives.

7. Give the Accus. Plur. of the three Reflexive Pronouns.

8. Translate—They perceived that he was faithful to them; send whomsoever you wish; I must do it myself; he said that the barbarians were hostile.

9. Translate—εἰ γὰρ ταῦτα γένοιτο. ἔστιν οἳ λέγουσι. αἰσχύνομαι λέγων. αἰσχύνομαι λέγειν. τῷ ὄντι.

68.

1. Fut. Indic. of ἁμαρτάνω, φράζω, νομίζω, τελέω, θνήσκω.

2. Write out Imper. and Opt. Aorist Act. of πράττω.

3. Decline Δημοσθένης, Ἡρακλῆς.

4. Parse ἐπίσταται, τεθῆναι, δέδοται, καθελεῖν, ἐκβῶσι.

5. Distinguish the meanings of θνήσκειν, θανεῖν, τεθνηκέναι. ἔστην, ἔστησα, ἔστηκα.

6. Why is Gen. Absolute less common in Greek than Abl. Absolute in Latin?

7. Gen. Sing. and Dat. Plural of χρυσοῦς, ἁπλοῦς, ταχύς, εὐγενής.

8. Translate—He asked if this was true; he said he would do nothing against the law; they persuaded him to give them money; it is plain that they are preparing.

9. Translate—τὰ ἔπειτα. εἴθε σὺ φίλος γένοιο. χαλεπῶς ἔχει ὑπὸ τραυμάτων τινῶν. ἤροντο αὐτόν τί καὶ βουλόμενος ταῦτα πράττοι.

69.

1. Write out Pres. Indic. of ἵημι, εἰμί, εἶμι.

2. Decline αἰδώς, φρέαρ.

3. Parse in two ways ἕδρα, πείσομαι, ποιήσει.

4. Pres. Infin. of ζάω, ἐρωτάω, μισθόω, ἡγέομαι, δείκνυμι.

5. Give the Correlatives of ποῦ.

6. Explain Definite and Indefinite Temporal Clauses.

7. Distinguish αὐτῷ, αὑτῷ. ταὐτῷ, τούτῳ. σφῶν, σφῶν.

8. Translate—At whose bidding did you come?

if you wish I will do this; he stood in the middle of the road; they crossed before the others answered.

9. Translate—καλῶς ἔχει. οὐκέτι οἱοί τ᾽ ἦσαν τὸν γέλωτα κατέχειν. ἦγε στρατιὰν ὅτι πλείστην. μὴ γένοιτο.

70.

1. Principal Tenses of ἀφίημι, ἀνοίγνυμι.

2. Gen. Sing. and Dat. Plural of μοῖρα, πέλεκυς, ἀστήρ, πῦρ, δένδρον.

3. Parse ᾔδεῖτο, εἶα, μεθέξετε, ἀπήλασε, ἔφθη.

4. Classify the Consonants.

5. How is the want of a Third Personal Pronoun supplied? Give examples.

6. Name the Prepositions governing one case. Give meaning of each.

7. Distinguish ἡ, ἤ, ᾗ, ἥ, ᾖ.

8. Translate—δῆλοι ἦσαν ἀποροῦντες. οὐ δύναμαι μὴ οὐ λέγειν. ταῦτα ἐγένετο. ταῦτα ἐγένετο ἄν. ταῦτα γένοιτο ἄν.

9. Translate—We know you are wise; he said he would not remain; he took the money and went; surely you will not send that slave.

71.

1. Write out Fut. Indic. Act. of ἐλαύνω, σφάλλω.
2. Gen. Sing. and Dat. Plural of ἵλεως, εὔχαρις, ἄπους.
3. Aorist Indic. Act. of ἁλίσκομαι, ἐμπίπτω, τυγχάνω, μεθίημι, ἐάω.
4. How is the Nom. Sing. formed in Consonant Stems of Third Declension?
5. Principal Tenses of πυνθάνομαι, θνήσκω, μανθάνω.
6. Meaning of αἱρέομαι, μεταπέμπομαι, ἡγέομαι, ἀξιόω, ἀνάγομαι.
7. What is meant by Protasis, Apodosis?
8. Translate—ἀλγεῖν τοὺς πόδας. ὀξὺν θάνατον ἀποθνήσκειν. πάλαι οἶδα. ὡς εἰπεῖν. οὐχ οἷόν τ᾽ ἐστί.
9. Translate—They agreed (ὁμολογέω) owing to the corn having failed (ἐπιλείπω); it was announced that the allies had been defeated (ἡττάω).

72.

1. Name Verbs that take a double Augment.
2. Perf. Indic. Act. of φέρω, ὁράω, γίγνομαι, ἐγείρω, πίπτω.

3. Decline in Plural λεώς, ἥρως.

4. Write out Aorist Imper. of βάλλω, γίγνομαι.

5. Parse εἶα, ἔζη, ἐξείλον, ἀπόκριναι, ἀπήλασε.

6. Construct a Conditional Sentence in which the Subjunctive would be correctly used.

7. Derive ἄροτον, γεωργός, ἄσβεστος, κρατήρ, λήθη.

8. Translate—τὸ ὑπὸ βαρβάρων νενικῆσθαι. πῶς ἂν ὀλοίμην. ἄλλως τε καί. οὐ γὰρ φιλικῶς εἶχον οἱ βάρβαροι.

9. Translate—He said (ἔφη) that they were Athenians, but that he himself was a Persian; he was not willing to go till (πρίν) his wife persuaded him.

73.

1. Fut. Indic. of ἀποκτείνω, γίγνομαι, διδάσκω, ὁράω, μεθίημι.

2. Explain the formations of Strong and of Weak Perfects, of Strong and of Weak Aorist Act.

3. Compare ἄφθονος, ὄψιος, μέγας, πολύς, αἰσχρός.

4. Write out Aorist Indic. Act. and Middle of τίθημι.

- 5. Principal Tenses of ἔχω, θάπτω.

6. Explain "Attraction of Relative". Give example.

7. Decline in Sing. μέλι, γῆρας.

8. Translate—Whoever does this is worthy to be punished; such a man as you; they perceived he was friendly to them; we must do it ourselves.

9. Translate—πράγματα εἶχον ὑπὸ τῶν λῃστῶν. εἰ ἦλθες ἐθαύμασα ἄν. αὐτὴ ἐφ ἑαυτῆς ἡ πόλις ἐγένετο. μὴ γένοιτο. οὐκ ἂν γένοιτο.

74.

1. Aorist Indic. of ἀρκέω, ἐάω, ἀναβοάω, ἐκπλέω, ὄμνυμι.

2. Nom. Sing., Gender and English of κύνας, κρέα, δορί, κλεῖς.

3. Parse ἑάλω, ἀπέδρα, εἴρηται, ἠκηκόει, ἤρετο.

4. Write out Aorist Subj. Act. of δίδωμι, τίθημι.

5. What is the construction of Final Clauses?

6. Give examples of Partitive Genitive, Cognate Accusative.

7. Acc. Sing. and Dat. Plural of βαρύς, σαφής, πλείων.

8. Translate—They escaped before they were

judged; he did not land the soldiers till (πρίν) these ships came; although he perceived this he was silent.

9. Translate (with Notes)—οἱ ἀπὸ τῶν πύργων οὐκ ἔβαλλον. ἤρετο τίνος δεόμενος ἥκοι. ἄλλοι τε καὶ Θεραμένης. εἰ τοῦτα ποιήσειας, ἀδικήσειας ἄν.

75.

1. Write out Weak Aorist Indic. Middle of ἄρχω.

2. Nom. and Gen. Sing. of ἐρήμοις, ἐγκεκυφότες, λειφθεισῶν, ζώσης, ἐφεστῶσιν.

3. Principal Tenses of καλέω, γιγνώσκω.

4. Decline ὅστις.

5. Parse ἔσταμεν, ἀφείμην, ἐπιτιθῶμεν, μεθῆκεν, ἐπίοντι.

6. How is a Wish expressed with reference to Past, Present, and Future Time?

7. Aorist Indic. of ὁράω, φέρω, ἔχω, καίω, πάσχω.

8. Translate—If he were to do this, he would be worthy of death; such conduct is disgraceful; those who do not obey will be punished; no one either saw or heard.

9. Translate (with Notes)—σὺν τοῖς θησαυροῖς οἷς ὁ πατὴρ κατέλιπεν. οὐκ ἂν δύναιο παντ᾽ ἔχειν ἃ μή σε δεῖ.

76.

1. Parse ἔγημε, ἕσπετο, σχεῖν, πεσεῖ, ἔασον.
2. Decline υἱός.
3. Weak Aorist Indic. Pass. of λαμβάνω, σώζω, τελέω, τρέφω.
4. Explain "Assimilation". Give examples.
5. Write out Pres. Indic. Act. of ἐάω, διψάω.
6. Derive Syllable, Parallel, Physiology, Comet, Planet.
7. Greek for—80, 900, 26, 8th, 70th.
8. Translate—Whomsoever they found they killed; do not write that; at my bidding he went away; they sailed while it was yet night.
9. Translate (with Notes)—οἱ μὲν ἐπορεύοντο τὸ πλῆθος ὡς δισχίλιοι. ἀφηγεῖτο ὅπως μὴ πλανῶνται αἱ ἑπόμεναι νῆες.

77.

1. Write out Imperf. Indic. Act. of θέω, βοάω.
2. Nom. Sing., Gender and English of γονάσι, ἄστη, τριχός, ἀστράσι, ἐτῶν.

3. Perf. Indic. Pass. of ἐλαύνω, ἁρπάζω, δοκέω, γίγνομαι, καλέω.

4. Parse σφᾶς, του, ἅττα, ὅτῳ, ἅττα.

5. Principal Tenses of διδάσκω, εὑρίσκω.

6. What case in Greek corresponds to the Latin Ablative?

7. Decline in Sing. πρᾶος.

8. Translate—He would have been willing, if he had known; if ever death comes, no man is willing to die; would that you had not come.

9. Translate—δίκαιός εἰμι εἰπεῖν. ἴσασι δὲ οὐδὲν ὧν λέγουσι. μὴ τοσόνδ᾽ ἔλθοι κακόν. τὸ πολὺ τῆς νήσου ἔλαθε κατακαυθέν.

78.

1. Write out Fut. Indic. of τείνω, πνέω.

2. Decline in Sing. ὀξύς, ἀσθενής.

3. Give the Participles Middle and Pass. of λαμβάνω.

4. Distinguish ἤρετο, ᾔρετο. ἠρᾶτο, ᾑρεῖτο.

5. Show the construction of an Indirect Question.

6. Parse ἠνέθη, δυνήσει, κέλευσον, τρωθείη, καλλίω.

7. Gen. and Dat. Sing. of προδότης, νεότης, κέρδος, πόνος, φροντίς, μάντις.

8. Translate—I gave him wine to drink; when he heard what had happened, he was silent; they set up a trophy, which stands in the middle of the plain.

9. Distinguish οἱ οὐ ποιοῦντες, οἱ μὴ ποιοῦντες. μέλει, μέλλει. φαίνομαι ποιεῖν, φαίνομαι ποιῶν. τὸν δοῦλον αὐτοῦ, τὸν αὐτοῦ δοῦλον.

79.

1. Fut. Indic. of κηρύττω, φθείρω, βιβάζω, αἱρέω, ὄμνυμι.

2. Principal Tenses of θνήσκω, πάσχω.

3. Form Nom. Sing. from the Stems ἀνδριαντ-, κανον-, τερματ-, οἰκητορ-, μερες-.

4. Parse ἐκτεθείη, καθῆσειν, ἐφίεσθαι, συνέθεντο, ἐρράγη.

5. Compare πένης, ἀλγεινός, ἄνω, ἥσυχος, πικρός.

6. Write out Weak Aorist Imper. Act. and Middle of παύω.

7. Greek for—to take, to be taken; to kill, to be killed; to banish, to be banished; to die, to be dead.

8. Translate—εἰ ἐπεγένετο πνεῦμα οὐκ ἂν διέφυγον. διαλαθὼν ἐσέρχεται εἰς τὴν Μυτιλήνην.

9. Translate—He asked upon what terms they would become allies; they bade him take whomsoever he wished; he has been ill (νοσέω) for ten days.

80.

1. Write out Pres. Opt. Act. of ὁράω, and Aorist Opt. Middle of δέχομαι.

2. Nom. and Gen. Sing. of κλίμακας, πείρας, ὁπλίσει, πλίνθους, ὅρκων.

3. Parse ἔτλην, ὑπομείνας, φανῆναι, νικῷεν, ὄληται.

4. Decline ὄρνις, γῆρας.

5. Principal Tenses of ζεύγνυμι, ἐγείρω.

6. Distinguish ἄττα, ἄττα. αὐτούς, αὐτούς. αὗται, αὐταί. σφῷν, σφῶν.

7. Give rule for forming Weak Aorist of Liquid Verbs.

8. Translate — ἐκέλευον αὐτόν τὸ ἐπὶ σφᾶς εἶναι ἐπιχειρεῖν. τούτων ζῶντες ἐκομίσθησαν ὀκτὼ ἀποδέοντες τριακόσιοι.

9. Translate—If he had obeyed me, he would now be living; would that he had not written this; I fear he will not come.

81.

1. Write out Imperat. Pres. of ἐάω, λογίζομαι.
2. Decline in Plur. χείρ, πῦρ.
3. Perf. Indic. Act. of ἔχω, πίπτω, συγκρύπτω, φαίνω, τίθημι.
4. English of ἐνταῦθα, ὅθεν, πόσος, ἡνίκα, ποθέν.
5. Parse εἰδεῖεν, πρεστηκόσι, ἀναχθείς, εἰρήσθω, πύθῃ.
6. Classify the Consonants.
7. Give examples of construction and meaning of πρός, διά.
8. Translate—Whenever he fights, he conquers; would that he might be saved; he came of his own accord; on the top of the wall.
9. Translate (with Notes)—μεγάλῃ τῇ φωνῇ εἶπε. οὐ μὴ γένηται τοῦτο. ἔφθην ἀφίκομενος. ἐκ τοῦ ἴσου μαχοῦνται.

82.

1. Infinitives (all Tenses) Middle and Passive of καλέω.
2. Principal Tenses of ἀφικνέομαι, βαίνω.
3. Gen. Sing., Gender and English of ὄρος, ὅρος, γέρας, γῆρας, μέριμνα, θαῦμα.

4. How are Verbs classified according to the formation of Present Stem ?

5. Write out Aorist Opt. of σιωπάω, δέχομαι.

6. Show the construction of a Negative Command, Direct and Indirect.

7. Decline in Plur. ὑγιής.

8. Translate—They used to do whatever he ordered; they answered that (ὅτι) they would not do this; consider how you will do this.

9. Translate—πρός τινος λέγειν. ὡς ἐπὶ τὸ πολύ. παρὰ μικρόν. εὖ σοι γένοιτο. ὅς οὐ λέγει. ὅστις μὴ λέγει.

83.

1. Pres. Infin. of χράομαι, ὁράω, ζάω, αἰδέομαι, ἵημι.

2. Point out peculiarities in Declension of ὄρνις, πούς, ὕδωρ.

3. Write out Imperf. and Aor. Indic. Act. of τίθημι.

4. Explain Oxytone, Paroxytone, Perispomenon, Enclitic.

5. Distinguish the meaning of Aorist and Present in each Mood.

6. Parse ἆραι, ᾐτιῶντο, ἠγωνίσω, παρέντι, σφήλαντι.

7. Derive ἐκεχειρία, φάσμα, ἄπορος, ὁλκός, ὅμαιμος.

8. Distinguish καθαίρω, καθαιρέω. ἀπορέω, ἀπορρέω. οὔκουν, οὐκοῦν. οἷος, οἶος, οἰός. πάρα, παρά. πῶς, πως.

9. Translate—He said he did not know whither they were going to sail; do not accept these gifts; they used the man as a messenger.

84.

1. Give the meanings of πέποιθα, πέπεικα, πέπραγα, πέπραχα, ὅλωλα, ὤλεσα, ἔστην, ἔστησα.

2. Nom. and Gen. Sing. and English of πυρά, ὠσί, κρέα, ἦρι.

3. Strong Fut. Indic. Pass. of θάπτω, φθείρω, φαίνω, ῥήγνυμι, στέλλω.

4. Parse εἴη, εἴη, ᾔει, ἵῃ, ἴῃ.

5. Principal Tenses of ἁμαρτάνω, ὄλλυμι.

6. In what Clauses is μή regularly used?

7. Parse ὅτου, ἄττα, ἅττα, σφῶν, αὗται.

8. Translate—If they had remained, they would have died; they made a truce on these terms; if ever I am convicted (ἐλέγχω), I confess I should justly be put to death.

9. Translate (with Notes)—ἔξεστί σοι μεθ' ἡμῶν

γενομένῳ μηδένα δεσπότην ἔχοντα ζῆν. ὁρᾷς τἀμὰ
πράγματ᾽ ὡς ἔχει. ποταμὸς Κύδνος ὄνομα.

85.

1. Write out Aorist Imperative of λαμβάνω,
γίγνομαι.

2. Compare ἀληθής, αἴδοιος, ὀλίγος, μακρός.

3. Aorist Indic. of πυνθάνομαι, ἐλαύνω, τείνω,
κάμνω, ἀμφιέννυμι.

4. Derive Doxology, Rhinoceros, Eclipse, Gym-
nastic, Atom.

5. Compare the formation of Strong and Weak
Tenses.

6. Parse γεγῶτες, ὤνησας, ὤκεις, γαμεῖς, δρῶσα.

7. Gen. Sing. and Gender and English of φῶς,
σκάφος, πόσις, τέρας, τάφρος.

8. Translate—We must bear, though it is hard
to bear (δύσφορος); they perceived that the barbarians were unfriendly to them.

9. Translate—ῥᾷον γὰρ τὴν φυλακὴν ἐλάνθανον
ὅποτε πνεῦμα ἐκ πόντου εἴη. Κῦρος φίλων ᾤετο
δεῖσθαι.

86.

1. Imperf. Indic. of συλλέγω, ἑστιάω, ἀνέχομαι,
ἀθυμέω, αἱρέω.

2. Decline in Sing. μοῖρα, εἰκών.

3. Infinitives and Participles Act. of εὑρίσκω.

4. Gen. Sing. and Dat. Plural of γλυκύς, ἀξιό-χρεως.

5. Principal Tenses of κρίνω, αἰσθάνομαι.

6. Distinguish νεῷ, νέῳ. ἐᾶν, ἐάν. ἀπιών, ἀπών.

7. What is meant by Graphic or Vivid Sequence?

8. Translate—He asked whether any man was wiser than I; they saw that the enemy was coming upon (ἐπεῖμι) them.

9. Translate—εἴθ' ηὕρομέν σε μὴ λυπουμένην. οὐκ ἂν δυναίμην. ὦ τλῆμον, οὐκ οἶσθ' οἱ κακῶν ἐλήλυθας.

87.

1. Write out Pres. Indic. Act. of στεφανόω, πεινάω.

2. Nom. and Gen. Sing., Gender and English of κλίμακας, τάφρῳ, σκότους, σάρκας, ἔῳ.

3. Fut. Indic. of πλέω, ὄλλυμι, ἐθέλω, εὑρίσκω, τρέχω.

4. Explain Crasis, Coronis, Diaeresis.

5. Parse εἴασε, ἤρετο, ἐδῄου, ἐδέδισαν, ἐδίδοσαν.

E

6. Distinguish the meanings of Present and Aorist (1) in Indic., (2) in Opt.

7. What is the force of ἄν occurring in a Principal Sentence ?

8. Translate—He said he wanted to know how many they were; when this took place, he happened to be in Athens.

9. Translate—σοί γε μέντοι φίλοι γενέσθαι περὶ παντὸς ἂν ποιησαίμεθα. ἀναμνήσω ὑμᾶς τὰ τούτῳ πεπραγμένα.

88.

1. Principal Tenses of λανθάνω, μανθάνω.

2. Name Feminine words in -ος of Second Declension.

3. Aorist Indic. Pass. of καλέω, ἀνάγω, ἀποφέρω, ἐξωθέω, αἱρέω.

4. Write out Imperf. Indic. of εἶμι and ἵημι.

5. Nom. and Gen. Sing., Gender and English of κρᾶτα, ὤτων, ὀργὰς, θρόνων.

6. Parse in two ways ἴσθι, ἔστησαν, τοῦ, τιμῶσι.

7. Show the construction of Definite and Indefinite Relative Clauses.

8. Translate—Do not shut the gate till I come; he was chosen general with nine others; if he were to do this, he would be worthy of death.

9. Translate (with Notes)—πατρὸς γὰρ ταῦτα ἐδεξάμην πάρα. ὁ δε οὐκ ἔφη δέξεσθαι τοὺς ὅρκους ἐὰν μὴ ὀμνύωσι.

89.

1. Parse παρειλήφει, φείσεσθε, μεθῆκε, ἔδῃου, τεθναίη.

2. Write out Pres. Subj. Act. of δηλόω, δίδωμι.

3. Decline κλείς and ναῦς.

4. Perf. Indic. Act. of μένω, πλέω, καλέω, γιγνώσκω, φέρω.

5. Show various ways of expressing " Purpose " in Greek.

6. Parse σέθεν, νίν, σφίσι, ὅτοις.

7. Greek for—on horseback; beyond one's power; all day long; equally; as quickly as possible.

8. Translate—ποιείτω τοῦτο ὁ βουλόμενος. πῶς ἔχεις χρημάτων ; ποῖ τράπωμαι ; μείζων ἢ κατ᾽ ἄνθρωπον.

9. Translate—I will not cease trusting him as long as I live; he bade us remain there till the messenger returned.

90.

1. Decline in Sing. ἔρις, φύσις.

2. Parse τραπῶμαι, ἀνάσχου, παρῄνει, ἴστω, ὑφειμένην.

3. Give the Dative Plural of all the Reflexive Pronouns.

4. Write out Pluperf. Indic. Pass. of γράφω, πλέκω.

5. Greek for—21st, 70, 80, 2000, nine times.

6. Decline in Plural βραχύς.

7. Write out the Aorist εἶπον.

8. Translate—He said he would not give anything to any one; these men died that we might be saved.

9. Translate—διωκτέον ἡμῖν τὴν ἀρετήν. οὐ μὴ ποτ᾽ ἔλθω. δῆλοι ἦσαν ἀποροῦντες. λέγεις ἀκοῦσαι μαλθάκα.

91.

1. Write out Perf. Indic. Act. of ἴστημι, and Aorist Indic. Middle of ἵημι.

2. Dat. Sing. and Plur. of βωμός, ἕξις, χιτών, λέχος.

3. Principal Tenses of πυνθάνομαι, τυγχάνω.

4. Acc. Sing. and Dat. Plur. of δοκῶν, νικῶν, δηλῶν.

5. Infinitives and Participles Active of ἐλαύνω.

6. Show the constructions of ὥστε.

7. Perf. Indic. Pass. of ἔχω, ἄρχω, ἐργάζομαι, λαμβάνω, τέμνω.

8. Translate—Who is there who does not perceive? some fled one way, some another; he sent for an army in addition to the one that he had.

9. Show the force of the Prepositions in ἀναχωρεῖν, ἀπεργάζεσθαι, διαφέρειν, καταγελᾶν, περιγίγνεσθαι, μετατιθέναι.

92.

1. Aor. Indic. Act. of ἀπελαύνω, αἰνέω, κατακαίω, ἀποκτείνω.

2. Decline in Plural ὅστις, ἑαυτόν.

3. Parse ἐκταθήσεται, ἀφείθησαν, ἡγείσθω, ἐπήροντο, ἔα.

4. Nom. Sing., Gender and English of χωρίων, ἀκοντιστάς, ῥοῦ, ἠπείρῳ, χρῷ.

5. Write out Optative and Imperative Weak Aorist Passive of λείπω.

6. Distinguish νέων, νεῶν. εἰδῆτε, ἴδητε. ὅτε, ἐπεί.

7. Show the force of ἄν in a Clause.

8. Translate—If we do this, we shall conquer; he fled without our knowing; he perceived that he had fallen; wait till I come.

9. Translate—καὶ μὴν ἁμαρτήσει γε μὴ δράσας τάδε. πολλάκις μὲν ἡδέως ἂν ἴδοιμι αὐτὸν μὴ ὄντα ἐν ἀνθρώποις.

93.

1. Write out Fut. Indic. Act. of ἐλαύνω, κρίνω.

2. Principal Tenses of ὁράω, φέρω.

3. Nom. Sing., Gender and English of πόσεως, γειτόνων, μάρτυσι, δικαστῇ.

4. Parse ἐπίστασαι, ἀνήσομεν, ἐκβῶσι, ἀπῆραν, εἰδέναι.

5. Aorist Indic. of ἀποδιδράσκω, ἀναβαίνω, εἰσφέρω, αἰσθάνομαι, ἀνοίγνυμι.

6. Show the construction of Verbs of *fearing*.

7. Derive ψηφίζομαι, ἀκτή, ῥαψῳδός, εὐήμερος, μοῖρα.

8. Translate—He sent forward 100 men, that whenever the gate was opened they might run in; he demanded that the cities should be given up to him; owing to his unwillingness.

9. Translate (with Notes)—ἴσασιν οὐδὲν ὧν λέγουσι. ὡς ἔπος εἰπεῖν. πολλ' ἂν σὺ λέξας οὐδὲν ἂν πλέον λάβοις.

94.

1. Write out Aorist Subj. and Imperat. of ἔχω.

2. Decline in Sing. ὁ αὐτός.

3. Fut. Indic. of μάχομαι, πίπτω, καίω, ἔχω, καθίημι.

4. Derive Evangelist, Drama, Paralysis, Crystal, Catastrophe.

5. Parse ἔασον, ζώης, ἆραι, κωλῦσαν, ἀνεκόπη.

6. Show the construction of Consecutive Clauses, with Negatives.

7. Gen. Sing. and Dat. Plural of ἥρως, χείρ, υἱός, οὖς, βότρυς.

8. Translate—They did not come till they heard; they fled before being judged; you are the cause (αἴτιος) of very many having perished.

9. Translate (with Notes)—χαίρω ᾗ ἔγραψας ἐπιστολῇ. ἐπαινῶ οἷόν σε ἄνδρα. οὐκ εἶδεν οὐδείς. οὐδεὶς οὐκ εἶδεν. αὐτή ταδ᾽ εἵλου.

95.

1. Infinitives and Participles of νομίζω.

2. Nom. and Dat. Plural of γνούς, βαλών, βεβοηθηκώς, νικῶν.

3. Principal Tenses of δοκέω, λέγω.

4. Point out peculiarities in Declension of δένδρον, ὄνειρος, δόρυ.

5. Write out Imperf. Act. and Middle of τίθημι.

6. Show the construction of Temporal Clauses, Definite and Indefinite.

7. Explain Assimilation, Metathesis.

8. Translate—Ζεῦ, μὴ λάθοι σε τῶνδ' ὅς αἴτιος κακῶν. πάντες τιμωρώμεθα τοὺς ἄνδρας ἀνθ' ὧν ὑβρίσθημεν.

9. Translate—He asked how many he was to take; they were afraid that he would make war on them.

96.

1. Fut. Indic. of γαμέω, βλώσκω, βοάω, γιγνώσκω, ὄμνυμι.

2. Decline in Sing. γῆρας, ἔαρ, γόνυ.

3. Parse ἐξενωμένοις, ἔσοιτο, λογίζον, μισθοῦσθαι, ἐρράγη.

4. Distinguish παρά, πάρα. σίγα, σῖγα. θέων, θεῶν. ἤ, ἥ.

5. Show the constructions of πρίν.

6. Write out Imperf. of φημί, Pluperf. of οἶδα.

7. How is the Nominative of Third Declension formed from the Stem?

8. Translate—If I had asked, he would have answered; if you were to become rich, what would you lack (δέω)?

9. Translate (with Notes)—ὅσοι δὲ γαλήνῃ (in calm weather) κινδυνεύσειαν ἠλίσκοντο. κατθανὼν ἂν ἀπώλετο. τοῦ σ᾽ ἀποστερῶ;

97.

1. Write out Imperf. Indic. Act. of ἐάω, ζάω.

2. Name the Prepositions governing one case.

3. Parse συνεθέμεθα, ἀφέθησαν, μεθεῖτο, εἰδείη, ἴστω.

4. Principal Tenses of καίω, μάχομαι.

5. Show various methods of asking a Direct Question in Greek.

6. Point out peculiarities in Declension of σκότος, ἧπαρ, Περικλῆς.

7. Give Active and Middle meanings of μισθόω, λανθάνω, ἵημι, γαμέω, δανείζω.

8. Translate—I seize him by the hand; they are unskilled (ἄπειρος) in this art; where on earth? I suffer the same things as you (do).

9. Translate—εἰ ἀπήλασα αὐτόν μᾶλλον ἂν μ᾽ ἐπῄνεσας. ἐπεμελεῖτο ὅπως μὴ ἄσιτοι ἐσοῖντο.

98.

1. Parse ἀπηνέχθη, τεθνᾶσι, παρῄνει, ἀπέδρα, κατειλήφεσαν,

2. Form and compare Adverbs from ταχύς, φρόνιμος, ῥᾴδιος.

3. Write out Pres. Indic. of αἰτιάομαι, πλέω.

4. Explain the forms θρίξ, ἐτύθην, βέβληκα, τείνω, λέων.

5. Decline in Sing. ἄχθος, κρέας.

6. Write out Fut. Indic. of εἰμί and ἐλαύνω.

7. Enumerate the chief uses of the Subjunctive in Dependent Clauses.

8. Translate (with Notes on the Moods)—ἐγὼ γὰρ ὀκνοίην μὲν ἂν εἰς τὰ πλοῖα ἐμβαίνειν ἃ ἡμῖν δοίη, μὴ ἡμᾶς αὐταῖς ταῖς τριήρεσι καταδύσῃ.

9. Translate—He said that they bade him count (ἀριθμέω) how many men there were in the market-place.

99.

1. Strong Aorist Indic. Pass. of πήγνυμι, καίω, κλέπτω, ἐκπλήττω, πίνω.

2. Infinitives and Participles Active of τέμνω.

3. Parse ὅτου, αὐτοῖς, σφίσι, ἄττα.

4. Which Negative is used in Final, Causal, Conditional, and Relative Clauses?

5. Principal Tenses of μένω, πίπτω.

6. Nom. and Gen. Sing., Gender and English of σίτων, κόραις, θάμβει, ὁλκάσι.

7. Explain formation of Present Stem in στάζω, βάπτω, βάλλω, τυγχάνω.

8. Translate (with Notes)—οὐ μὴ ποιήσεις. οὐ μὴ ποτ᾽ ἔλθω. ταῦτα ἅ ἐστί σοι λελεγμένα. ἐν τῷ πρὸ τοῦ χρόνῳ.

9. Translate—For the future; he received this as a gift; he received this gift; if you had not come, you would not have seen.

100.

1. Distinguish ἐφίσταμαι, ἐπίσταμαι, μέλει, μέλλει, ἤρετο, ᾔρετο.

2. Greek for—8th, 70th, 80th, 200, 2000.

3. Classify Verbs according to the formation of Present Stem.

4. Show the construction and meanings of πρός, μετά, διά.

5. Parse ἀπεχθήσει, ἀφῄρει, ἠνέσχετο, ἐνόν, ἵει.

6. Nom. and Gen. Sing., Gender and English of δέμας, θρόνων, κρατί, ὀνείδεσι.

7. How is an Indirect Statement expressed in Greek?

8. Translate—ὡς ὤφελε τοῦτο ποιεῖν. τί παθὼν οὕτω ταχὺς ἀπῆλθε; ἄλλως ἄρ᾽ ὑμᾶς, ὦ τέκν᾽, ἐξεθρεψάμην.

9. Translate—We have come in order to see; they escaped before they were judged; they perceived that he was friendly to them.

101.

1. Write out Aorist Opt. and Imperative Act. of ἀγγέλλω.

2. Nom. and Gen. Sing., Gender and English of γόνασι, ἤρῳ, ἦρος, κρέα, εὐνάς.

3. Aorist Indic. Middle of ὄλλυμι, ἀνάγω, αἱρέω, ἀπεχθάνομαι, ἔχω.

4. Distinguish meanings of ὁρμίζω, ὁρμέω, ὁρμάω. ηὐξῆσθαι, εὔξασθαι. τεθνάναι, θανειν. σιγᾶν, σιγῆσαι.

5. Parse πίει, ἐκάην, μείνας, ἐρρύη, ἐνεγκάτω.

6. Explain Graphic or Vivid Sequence.

7. Give Active and Middle meaning of ἀμύνω, λανθάνω, ἅπτω, κομίζω.

8. Translate—Though he perceived this, he nevertheless observed (ἐμμένω) the truce; they spoke thus, but he answered as follows.

9. Translate—ὑμεῖς ἐστε παρ᾽ ὧν ἂν κάλλιστά τις τοῦτο μάθοι. οὐδεὶς ἐξὸν εἰρήνην ἄγειν πόλεμον αἱρήσεται.

102.

1. Perf. Indic. Act. of μιαίνω, διδάσκω, λαμβάνω, πάσχω, ὁράω.

2. Derive Genesis, Exodus, Heresy, Isosceles, Asylum.

3. Meaning of ἔφυν, ἔφυσα, πέφυκα, πέπραχα, πέπραγα.

4. Principal Tenses of πνέω, αἰνέω.

5. Parse μεθίστη, ἔστρωται, δεικνύσθων, ἔστασαν, ἑλῶσι.

6. Show the construction of Causal Clauses.

7. Gen., Gender and English of σκεῦος, ἄμπελος, στάχυς, κόρυς, πέλεκυς.

8. Translate—If he had done no wrong, you would have released him; if the king sends another general, I shall be willing to be friendly to you.

9. Translate—ἔφθη ποιήσας. οὐκ ἂν φθάνοις ποιήσας. ἐπὶ σοὶ ἔσται. χαρίζομαι οἵω σοὶ ἀνδρί. μαθὼν ἐμοῦ πάρα.

103.

1. Parse γνῶθι, ἁλῶναι, πείσεται, ἔαδον, ἠδεῖτο.

2. Write out Aorist Opt. and Subj. Act. of βαίνω.

3. Acc. and Gen. Sing. of μέγας, χρυσοῦς, ἀργυροῦς, πρᾶος.

4. Aorist Indic. Act. of διαβιβάζω, ἀπαίρω, ἐθίζω, ἐγείρω, γελάω.

5. Accent φυγειν, πεποιθεναι, ἐψευσμενος, λιπων, παρειχον, τιμησαι (Inf.).

6. Show the constructions of ὥστε.

7. Distinguish τοῦτο ἐγένετο. τοῦτο ἐγένετο ἄν. ἐνόσει, ἐνόσησε. γαμῶ, γαμοῦμαι. ἔλεγε τοιάδε. τοσαῦτα ἔλεξε.

8. Translate—They escaped observation more easily whenever there was a wind from the sea; they bade him make a truce with them.

9. Translate—ἠρώτων εἰ τι σφᾶς ἀγαθὸν δεδρακότες εἰσί. οὐδένι ὅτῳ οὐκ ἀπεκρίνατο. ὡς συνελόντι εἰπεῖν.

104.

1. Write out Fut. Indic. of βιβάζω, πίπτω.

2. Decline in Plural νεώς, ναῦς.

3. Principal Tenses of σπάω, ἁλίσκομαι.

4. Nom. and Acc. Plural of αὐτός, αὑτός, οὗτος, ὅστις.

5. Give examples of change of Stem Vowel occurring in Strong Aorist Passive.

6. Distinguish Genitive and Dative of Time. Give examples.

7. Show the construction of ὑπέρ, ὑπό.

8. Translate—They said that if we fought we should conquer; they said that if we had fought we should have conquered.

9. Translate—ἡμῖν δὲ ἐξὸν ζῆν μὴ καλῶς, καλῶς αἱρούμεθα μᾶλλον τελευτᾶν. ἔμοιγε νῦν τε καὶ πάλαι δοκεῖ.

105.

1. Fut. Indic. of κάμνω, πάσχω, αἰνέω, μανθάνω, ἀφίημι.

2. Parse χαλεπότητι, φυλακῇ, ἰσχύι, νιν, σέθεν.

3. Write out Pluperf. of οἶδα, Imperf. of εἰμι.

4. Parse βῇ, φθάσαι, ἀφίει, ἀνέδησαν, δέδασμαι.

5. Infinitives and Participles Active of ἵημι.

6. When can the Subjunctive be used in (1) Conditional Clauses, (2) Indirect Questions?

7. Distinguish ἡ ἐσχάτη νῆσος, ἐσχάτη ἡ νῆσος. πρὸς τούτοις. πρὸς ταῦτα. ὀλίγοι, οἱ ὀλίγοι. ἀμύνω, ἀμύνομαι.

8. Translate—ἄλλως ἔφη πονεῖν σφᾶς. φεύγειν φόνου. διὰ μακροῦ. τὸ ἔπειτα. τιμήσομαι.

9. Translate—We used to wait for the doors

to be opened, and as soon as the doors were opened we used to go in; all the Greeks perceived that you were wise.

106.

1. Write out Imperf. Indic. of οἴομαι, αἰτιάομαι.

2. Distinguish ὁρῶν, ὅρων, ὀρῶν. ἄγων, ἀγών. παρά, πάρα.

3. Principal Tenses of τελέω, ἀναλίσκω, ἀραρίσκω.

4. Infinitives and Participles Active of βαίνω.

5. Show the force of the termination in δικαστήριον, ῥῆμα, αὐλητρίς, νεότης, κρύβδην.

6. Parse ᾔεις, ἔστω, δόμενον, δεδίως, ἔσταμεν.

7. Show various ways of expressing a Final Clause.

8. Translate (with Notes)—καὶ μ' οὐ νομίζω παῖδα σὸν πεφυκέναι. οὐκ οἶσθα μοίρας ἧς τυχεῖν αὐτὴν χρεών ;

9. Translate—They said that otherwise (ἄλλως) they would not trust him; how would they ever arrive if they sailed the contrary way (εἰς τἀναντία) ?

107.

1. Write out Pres. Subj. Active of ὁράω, ζάω.

2. Decline in Sing. νεώς, θρίξ, ναῦς.

3. Perf. Indic. Pass. of τρέπω, σείω, κτάομαι, λαγχάνω, ἐλαύνω.

4. Give examples of the Dative of the Agent.

5. Parse παρῆκας, ἀπόκριναι, ἐνέσχετο, ἐθεάσω, ἔκεισο.

6. Give examples of a Conditional Sentence with Indic. and ἄν in the Apodosis.

7. Express in Greek in as many ways as possible, " I am able to do this ".

8. Translate (with Notes)—οὐκ οἶδ' ἂν εἰ πείσαιμι, πείρασθαι δὲ χρή. στρατόπεδον γὰρ δὴ τοῦτο κάλλιστον τῶν μέχρι τοῦδε συνῆλθεν.

9. Translate—If he comes he will see; if he were to come he would see; I was glad to hear this; you cannot do it too soon.

108.

1. Principal Tenses of βλώσκω, μιμνήσκω, τιτρώσκω.

2. Write out Pres. Indic. Act. and Imperf. Indic. Middle of ἀφίημι.

3. Nom. Sing., Gender and English of μέρει, σκότους, προφάσει, ὀνείρασι, δορί.

F

4. Aorist Indic. Act. of ἀνοίγνυμι, αὐξάνω, γαμέω, ἐάω, καλέω.

5. Distinguish ἱέναι, ἱέναι. ἴθι, ἴσθι. ἐπίστασθαι, ἐφίστασθαι. ᾖ, ῇ, ἤ.

6. Resolve the Crasis in ἄν, τἄν, κεἰ, χαἰ, οὔκ.

7. When is the Optative used in Conditional Clauses?

8. Translate (with Notes)—καὶ διαλεγόμενος αὐτῷ ἔδοξέ μοι ὁ ἀνὴρ εἶναι σοφός. ὡς εἰπεῖν ἄλλο οὐδὲν ἢ ἐκ γῆς ἐναυμάχησαν.

9. Translate—If you had asked, I should have answered ; surely you are not so foolish as to trust that man.

109.

1. Name Verbs in -αω that contract to -η instead of -α.

2. Write out Aorist Indic. Act. of γιγνώσκω, and Pluperf. Indic. Act. of θνήσκω.

3. Decline in Sing. πρᾶος, σῶς.

4. Parse ὁρμήσειε, ἐνόντα, διαφθείραντα, σποῦ.

5. Give example of Relative Clause with Final Sense.

6. Distinguish βαίνω, βιβάζω. ἔρχομαι, ἥκω. οἶδα, γιγνώσκω. οὐ μόνον, μόνον οὐ. πολιορκέω, ἐκπολιορκέω.

7. Point out peculiarities in Declension of γαστήρ, εἰκών, μάρτυς.

8. Translate—I know that I should be more vexed (ἄχθομαι) if this were to happen; this is the third year we have been at war.

9. Translate—τοῖς ἐρωτῶσι χαίρω ἀποκρινόμενος. ὅπως μὴ ἐρεῖς τοῦτο. φθάσας διέδραμε πρίν τινα κωλύειν.

110.

1. Perf. Indic. Act. of ἁμαρτάνω, ἐλαύνω, λαγχάνω, τέμνω, βαίνω.

2. Principal Tenses of ἀπεχθάνομαι, κάμνω.

3. Decline μνᾶ, γέρας.

4. Infinitives Active of γαμέω, φέρω.

5. Show the meaning and construction of διά, μετά.

6. Name Present Tenses having the force of a Perfect, and Perfect Tenses having the force of a Present.

7. Show the construction of an Indirect Statement.

8. Translate (with Notes)—θνήσκω παρόν μοι μὴ θανεῖν. ἀπαγορεύει ὑμῖν μὴ ἰέναι. ὁ ἀεὶ βασιλεύς.

9. Translate—He deserves to suffer this; he replied, with a laugh, as follows; you are evidently ill; we are at a loss how to act.

III.

1. Parse ἐνεγκάτω, ἑστῶτι, ἐπιστείλας, ἐνεκεκάλυπτο.

2. Fut. Indic. of ὀργίζομαι, θεάομαι, βοάω, οἴχομαι, γελάω.

3. Decline in Plural ὀστοῦν, νεώς, κέρας.

4. Write out Perf. Indic. Act. of ἵστημι.

5. Show the construction of an Indirect Question.

6. Distinguish οὐ and μή.

7. Gen. Sing. and Dat. Plural of τιμῶν, ἁπλοῦς, γλυκύς.

8. Translate (with Notes)—ὅπως ἔσεσθε ἄνδρες. εὐδαίμοσιν ὑμῖν ἔξεστι γίγνεσθαι. ἤκουσά του λέγοντος. μεγάλῃ τῇ φωνῇ ἀπεκρίνατο.

9. Translate—It was mainly for this reason that I wrote; I never saw him for five years; they were armed with the same weapons as Cyrus.

112.

1. Write out Aorist Subj. Act. of γιγνώσκω.

2. Principal Tenses of δάκνω, ἀνοίγνυμι, πίνω.

3. Derive Atom, Amnesty, Economy, Ecstasy, Catarrh.

4. How is a Wish expressed in Greek?

5. Parse ἀφείθην, ἔστάται, τεθήσεται, ἐῶεν, κεκτήμην.

6. Nom. Sing. (all Genders) of ἄττα, ὅτῳ, σφᾶς, αὗται, αὑταί.

7. What changes in the Stem Vowel regularly occur in forming Perfect Active?

8. Translate—Whenever any one pursued they did this; let us keep quiet till the messenger returns; whom are we to send?

9. Translate—πολλάκις δὴ οὕτω διετέθην ὥστε μοι δόξαι μὴ βιωτὸν εἶναι ἔχοντι ὡς ἔχω. διὰ τὸ ξένος εἶναι οὐκ ἂν οἴει ἀδικηθῆναι.

113.

1. Aorist Indic. of μάχομαι, ἀπόλλυμι, ῥήγνυμι, τιτρώσκω, μεθίημι.

2. Compare πέπων, πρῷος, εὐτελής, ἄφθονος.

3. Parse εἰώθει, ῥαγῆναι, προσθήσομεν, μέμνηται, κεκλῆο.

4. Participles of γίγνομαι, βούλομαι.

5. Distinguish πόσος, ὁπόσος, ποσός, τοσόσδε, ὅσος.

6. Show the construction of Direct and Indirect Command.

7. Explain the forms ἔσπεισμαι, ἐτέθην, πᾶσα, ἀνδρός.

8. Translate—They were inquiring whether this was true; would that I had seen; if he hears you he will obey.

9. Translate (with Notes)—οὐ γὰρ ἂν ἔφη βούλεσθαι ζῆν μὴ τιμωρήσας Μανίᾳ. ταύτην τὴν χώραν ἐπέτρεψε διαρπάσαι τοῖς Ἕλλησι.

114.

1. Write out Imperf. Indic. of χράομαι, πλέω.

2. Perf. Middle and Pass. of ὁράω, ἀνοίγνυμι, ἀμφιέννυμι, ῥήγνυμι.

3. Parse ἥττους, ἤθεσι, ἔνιοι, μεγέθους, ἀφανῆ.

4. Principal Tenses of ἀποκτείνω, ὄμνυμι.

5. Distinguish οὔτε, οὐδέ. αὐτόν, αὑτόν. εἴη, εἴη.

6. Show the construction of Consecutive Clauses.

7. Decline in Plural ὅστις, ἡδίων.

8. Translate—They evidently wished to remain

till the messenger came; he said he would not say anything; I envy (ζηλῶ) you your happiness.

9. Translate—δημοσίᾳ . . . ἰδίᾳ. βίᾳ πολιτῶν. ποῦ γῆς. ἀπὸ στόματος λέγειν. ἐξ ἴσου. πρὸ πολλοῦ ποιεῖσθαι.

115.

1. Name Verbs augmented like ἔχω.

2. Decline in Sing. πῆχυς, μάρτυς, αἰδώς.

3. Aorist Indic. Pass. of ὑποβάλλω, ἥδομαι, αἱρέω, εὑρίσκω, τίθημι.

4. Distinguish βουλή, ἐκκλησία. χειροτονέω, ψηφίζομαι. χιτών, χλαῖνα.

5. Write out Aorist Subj. Act. and Middle of δίδωμι.

6. Distinguish οἶος, οἷος. ἐρώτα, ἔρωτα. ηὐξῆσθαι, εὔξασθαι. ἤρετο, ᾔρετο. ἐφίστω, ἐπίστω.

7. Show by example that a Participle may be equivalent in meaning to (1) a Final, (2) a Concessive Clause.

8. Give (in Greek) the Direct Speech of —ἐκήρυξε βοηθεῖν ὅσοι ἐλεύθεροι εἶεν. ἀπεκρίνατο ὅτι μανθάνοιεν ἃ οὐκ ἐπίσταιντο.

9. Translate—We know you would have been happier if you had obeyed; we know you would be happier if you obeyed.

116.

1. Fut. Indic. of πλέω, πυνθάνομαι, τρέφω, τυγχάνω, ἁλίσκομαι.

2. Compare ἐγγύς, κάτω, εὔδιος, ἀλγεινός.

3. Principal Tenses of ῥήγνυμι, λαγχάνω, τείνω.

4. Distinguish ἄν in Apodosis (Principal Sentence) from ἄν in Protasis (Dependent Clause).

5. Write out Perf. Subj. and Opt. of κτάομαι.

6. Form Adjectives from φύσις, λίθος, αἰδώς, τλάω, χάρις, οὐρανός.

7. Show the meaning and construction of πρός and κατά.

8. Translate—τέθνηκα γὰρ τοὐπί σε. κακῶς ἀκούειν. ἔφευγε προδοσίας. ἀπέφυγε προδοσίας.

9. Translate—Do not conceal this from me; he touched my hand; they came to blows; we were annoyed at this.

117.

1. Imperf. Indic. Act. of ὠθέω, ὁράω, ἐάω, ἐθίζω, δυσαρεστέω.

2. Decline in Plural ἄστυ, βοῦς, ἔθνος.

3. Parse ἀνεμνήσθην, συνιῇ, οἴει, ἐλπίσαν, ἑωράκη.

4. Write out Pres. Subj. and Opt. Act. of δράω.

5. In what kinds of Sentence is μή used?

6. Show the force of the Preposition in ὑπο-βλέπω, περιγίγνεσθαι, ὑπερβάλλω, διαπράττω, ἀποδίδωμι, κατηγορέω.

7. Show the constructions of ὅπως.

8. Translate—ἔλεγε ἀκόντων ἐκείνων οὐκ ἂν προελθεῖν. ἑνὸς δέοντι τριακοστῷ ἔτει. διὰ τρίτης ἡμέρας.

9. Translate—I fear this will happen; I fear this will not happen; though they are not many, they will fight.

118.

1. Write out Pres. Opt. Act. of πλέω, τίθημι.

2. Decline in Sing. μνᾶ, λαγώς, μελί.

3. Perf. Indic. Act. of ἐάω, ἔχω, λανθάνω, πίνω, πίπτω.

4. Greek for—ipse, idem, ille, quis? se, unde.

5. Principal Tenses of τυγχάνω, ὄλλυμι.

6. Show the construction of Alternative Questions.

7. Parse μόνωπα, δαιτί, χροΐ, μέλη, κρεῶν.

8. Translate—τὸ ἐν Θετταλίᾳ ἐλάνθανεν αὐτῷ τρεφόμενον στράτευμα. περὶ παντὸς ἐποιεῖτο τούτους πλουσιωτέρους ποιεῖν.

9. Translate—He asked if there was any man wiser than I; we will not cease marching till we arrive at the place.

119.

1. Aorist Indic. of κερδαίνω, ἰλάσκομαι, ἀρέσκω, νέμω, ἐθέλω.

2. Acc. Sing. and Nom. Plural (all Genders) of ἐλάττοσι, σφαλεῖσι, ζῶντας, δηλοῦντας.

3. Parse ἐφθόνει, μάθωσι, τριψάτω, ἐνθυμήθητι, ᾤχου.

4. Write out Perf. Subj. and Opt. Middle of μιμνήσκω.

5. Derive Hemorrhage, Arctic, Obelisk, Heliotrope, Amethyst.

6. Show the various ways of expressing an Indirect Statement.

7. Distinguish Aorist and Present (1) in Indic., (2) in other Moods.

8. Translate—Some say that not even if you wished could you do this; it being in our power to live dishonourably, we choose rather to die honourably.

9. Translate (with Notes)—τὴν οὐσίαν ἣν κατέλιπε τῷ υἱεῖ οὐ πλείονος ἀξία ἐστί. δυνατώτεροι αὐτοὶ ἑαυτῶν ἐγένοντο.

120.

1. Principal Tenses of ἐγείρω, ὠθέω.

2. Form Abstract Nouns from σώφρων, παχύς, εὔνους, ἀληθής, εὐδαίμων.

3. Write out Pres. Indic. Act. of δέω (bind), and δέω (lack).

4. Classify the uses of αὐτός.

5. Parse δρῷημεν, ἥμενοι, ἐπῶρσεν, γέγηθε, πλήσειε.

6. Show the construction of a Deliberative Question, Direct and Indirect.

7. Nom. and Gen. Sing. and English of ἄνθρακας, χθόνα, κυσίν, θηρῶν, αὐχέσι.

8. Translate—They fought until the enemy sailed away; they did not cease fighting until the enemy sailed away.

9. Translate (with Notes)—τίνος ἂν δέοις μὴ οὐχὶ πάμπαν εὐδαίμων εἶναι; τὸν ἐξίοντα ἀεὶ οἱ ὑπηρέται συνέδουν.

121.

1. Write out Pres. Subj. Act. of βοάω, στεφανόω.

2. Decline in Plural ὕδωρ, οὖς, ὄρνις.

3. Parse καμῇς, ἐμπρησθείη, ἠφάνισε, γέρως, κατέαγα.

4. What kind of Verbs are followed by Genitive? Give examples.

5. Distinguish τὰ γενόμενα, τὰ ἂν γενομενα. οὐ μόνον, μόνον οὐ. οὐδέ, οὔτε.

6. How may Conditional Sentences be classified?

7. Show the meaning and construction of the Prepositions governing one case.

8. Translate—ἐπίσταται εἴ τις καὶ ἄλλος. οὐκ ὁρᾷς ἱν᾽ εἶ κακοῦ; φίλων ἄκλαυστος. ὀλοῦμαι μὴ μαθών.

9. Translate—He gave us water to drink; nobody said anything; he wished to know how many they were; whenever he said this they laughed.

122.

1. Fut. Indic. of τέμνω, φθείρω, χράομαι, φέρω, ἔχω, ἀφικνέομαι.

2. Parse ὅτω, αὗται, αὐτοῦ, ταύτῃ, νιν, σέθεν.

3. Write out Aorist Indic. Middle of ἀφίημι, Imperf. Indic. of εἰμι.

4. Positive of ἰσαίτατος, πλεῖστος, μείων, ἥττων, βέλτιστος, μαλιστα.

5. Distinguish οὐ and μή.

6. Form Verbs from ὅρος, χαλεπός, βαρύς, ἁγνός, εὐτυχής, ἔργον.

7. Explain Crasis, Elision, Assimilation.

8. Translate—ὅπως μοι μὴ ἐρεῖς. οὐ δύναμαι μὴ οὐ λέγειν. δίκαιός εἰμι τοῦτο πράττειν. παρὰ μικρὸν ἀποφεύγειν.

9. Translate—He was handsome in appearance and clever (δεινός) at speaking; they showed that they were ready; he would not be fighting now if he were not brave.

123.

1. Parse ἰοῦσαν, διαφθαρῇ, μέμνησαι, ἀπόκριναι, ἀγγεῖλαι.

2. Write out Fut. Indic. Act. and Middle of στέλλω.

3. Gen. Sing., Gender and English of σθένος, καιρός, γέρας, ἱμάς, φροντίς, μάντις.

4. Give example of Attraction of Relative.

5. Strong Aorist Indic. Pass. of ῥέω, τρέφω, καίω, ἄγνυμι, πήγνυμι.

6. Distinguish παρέις, παρείς. δήλοις, δηλοῖς. εἶναι, εἶναι. ποῖος, ποιός. παρά, πάρα.

7. Explain and give examples of Attic Reduplication.

8. Translate—The plaintiff; the defendant; to revolt from; to put out (to sea); to vote; the left wing; to pay the penalty.

9. Translate—If he did this he will be punished; we did not know where to go; he has been ruling these ten years.

124.

1. Principal Tenses of τρέχω, ῥέω, γίγνομαι.

2. Write out Pres. and Aorist Imperative Act. of ἵστημι.

3. Explain the formation of Nominative in χάρις, ποιμήν, γέρων, πούς.

4. Aorist Indic. of ἐάω, βοάω, μάχομαι, ἐπαινέω, ὄμνυμι.

5. Distinguish the meanings of ὅτε, ἐπεί, ὅταν.

6. Show the construction of ἕπομαι, μάχομαι, κατηγορέω, ὀργίζομαι.

7. Derive ἀκτή, ὁλκάς, σποράδην, οἰωνός.

8. Turn into Oratio Obliqua, after (1) ἔφη and (2) ἔλεξεν—εἰ ταῦτα ποιεῖ ἀδικεῖ. ἐὰν ταῦτα ποιήσῃ ἀδικήσει. εἰ ταῦσα ἐποίησε ἠδικήσεν ἄν.

9. Translate—Would that I had been present; he is not so wise as never to err; I fear he will not come.

125.

1. Mention Verbs that Augment ε to ει instead of η.

2. Derive Sarcophagus, Neuralgia, Cynic, Comma, Disastrous.

3. Parse ἡρῆσθαι, ᾤοντο, ἴασι, ἀναβαλοῦ, διακηκοώς.

4. Show by examples how the Temporal Conjunction "until" is expressed in Greek.

5. Acc. Sing. and Plural of ἁπλοῦς, μενῶν, ἡδίων, ἑστώς.

6. Give various equivalents of "nonne".

7. Distinguish Direct and Indirect Reflexives.

8. Translate (with Notes)—φοβοίμην ἂν τῷ ἡγεμόνι ᾧ δοίη ἕπεσθαι μὴ ἡμᾶς ἀγάγῃ ὅθεν οὐκ οἷόν τε ἔσται ἐξελθεῖν.

9. Translate—They ask us for food; I defend myself against my foes; he took me by the hand; you suffer the same things as I do.

126.

1. Fut. Indic. of τίκτω, πνέω, ἐλαύνω, ἀρκέω, πειράω.

2. Decline in Sing. ἥττων, δίπηχυς.

3. Principal Tenses of τέμνω, κλίνω, πάσχω.

4. Explain and give examples of "Compensatory Lengthening" (1) in Nouns, (2) in Verbs.

5. Parse γεγώς, ἆσσον, καθήσω, ξυνῆκα, σώθητι.

6. Give Rule for the treatment of Dependent Clauses in Oratio Obliqua.

7. Explain the meaning of ξενία, εὐφήμει, τύραννος.

8. Translate and give in Greek the Direct Speech—Τισσαφέρνης μὲν ὤμοσεν Αγεσιλάῳ εἰ σπείσαιτο ἕως ἔλθοιεν οὕς πέμψειε πρὸς βασιλέα ἀγγέλους διαπράξεσθαι αὐτῷ ἀφεθῆναι αὐτονόμους τὰς πόλεις.

9. Translate—I say you ought to cross the river before it is clear what the others are going to answer.

127.

1. Perf. Indic. Middle and Pass. of ὄμνυμι, φέρω, ἔχω, ἐγείρω, χέω, τίθημι.

2. Explain use of μή οὐ.

3. Write out Pres. Indic. of φημί, ἐπίσταμαι.

4. Gen. Sing. and Dat. Plural of ὄναρ, πρέσβυς, υἱός, οἶς, θρίξ.

5. Parse σκέψει, ἐροῦμεν, ἤρετο, ἐπρίω, τεθνάτω.

6. Show by example that a Participle may have the force of a Conditional Clause.

7. Derive and explain Ostracism, ψήφισμα.

8. Translate (with Notes)—προεῖπεν Ἀγησιλάω πόλεμον εἰ μὴ ἀπίοι. ἤδη ἦν ἀμφὶ ἀγορὰν πλή-θουσαν.

9. Translate—They said that if they had had arms they would have fought; this work is too difficult for us to do.

128.

1. Principal Tenses of νέμω, λανθάνω, δύναμαι.

2. Acc. Sing. and Nom. Plur. of αὐτός, οὗτος, ὅστις, φανῶν.

3. Show the construction of ὁμολογέω, πυνθάνο-μαι, φυλάττομαι.

4. Derive and explain μέλαθρον, κρατήρ, τραγῳ-δός, ἀλάστωρ.

5. Show how ἄν is used (1) in a Principal Sen-tence, (2) in Dependent Clauses.

6. Parse μεθεῖτο, ἐπίστασαι, ἐπιστῆσαι, φάνηθι, ἔπτατο.

7. How may " Yes " and " No " be expressed in Greek ?

8. Translate—οὐκ οἷός τ᾽ εἰμι μὴ οὐ λέγειν. οὐ μὴ γένηται τοῦτο. ἐπεὶ δε ὡς ἐκ τῶν δυνατῶν ἐτοῖμα ἦν.

G

9. Translate—Consider whether they seem to you to speak the truth; he said he did not know whether the ships were going to sail.

129.

1. Parse ἐᾶτε, κατακεῖσο, ζώης, ἀφιῆτε, ἐπιούσῃ.
2. Decline οἷς.
3. Write out Aorist Indic. Act. and Middle of μεθίημι.
4. Explain the construction of πρίν.
5. Distinguish the uses of the Subjunctive and Optative in Conditional Clauses.
6. Explain Metathesis, Syncope.
7. Distinguish χρῶ, χρῷ. ἔφρασα, ἔφραξα. πίων, πιών. λέλησμαι, λέλησμαι.
8. Translate—φόνου διώκειν. βαρβάρων Ἕλληνας ἄρχειν εἰκός. ἐν αἰτίᾳ εἶχον κατ᾽ ἀλλήλους πολλῇ τὸν Ἆγιν.
9. Translate—Nobody shall ever say that; silence is better than speech; she has black hair; would that I had died.

130.

1. Principal Tenses of ἐάω, αἰνέω, ἀκούω.
2. Decline ἥρως, πῦρ.

3. Distinguish the Active and Middle meanings of γράφω, τιμωρέω, μισθόω, δανείζω, φοβέω.

4. What parts of the Verb are Oxytone?

5. Parse in two ways πόσιν, ἔπαισε, αἰσθήσει.

6. Show the chief uses of the Subjunctive in Dependent Clauses.

7. How is " his " translated into Greek?

8. Translate—He said that if you had done this you would have been wrong; he said that if ever you did this you would be wrong.

9. Translate and give the Direct Speech in Greek of—ὑπέσχετο αὐτοῖς εἰ καλῶς καταπραξεῖεν ἐφ᾽ ἃ ἐστρατεύετο μὴ προσθεν παύσασθαι πρὶν αὐτοὺς ἐξάγοι οἴκαδε.

131.

1. Mention Compound Verbs taking the Augment before the Preposition.

2. Parse ἀηδές, κόραις, ὑψηλή, πραχθέν, ὄρη.

3. Show the construction of Verbals in -τεος.

4. Point out peculiarities in Declension of δεσμός, Σωκράτης, ὄρνις, εἰκών.

5. Show the chief uses of the Optative in Dependent Clauses.

6. Parse ψηφιεῖται, ἐλᾷ, ἀπιοῦσι, ἐπετόμην, ἐπετίμα.

7. Principal Tenses of καθίημι, σκεδάννυμι.

8. Translate—You are the cause of many having perished; I should be glad to see you; surely you are not foolish enough to trust him.

9. Translate—ἐκεῖνον καὶ σὺ ὁμολογεῖς ἐν τοῖς ἄριστον τῶν προτέρων εἶναι. ἐὰν μὲν ἑκών πείθηται, εἰ δὲ μὴ, κολάζουσι.

132.

1. Future Indic. of ·αἰδέομαι, εὑρίσκω, γιγνώσκω, δάκνω, ὑπισχνεομαι.

2. Explain Objective and Subjective Genitive. Give examples.

3. Give six Perfects having a Present meaning.

4. Acc. Sing., Dat. Plur. and English of μήν, σφραγίς, ὄναρ, δόρυ.

5. Principal Tenses of αὐξάνω, καίω, τείνω.

6. Greek for—7th, 9th, 50th, 60th, 80th, 500.

7. How may the Consonants be classified?

8. Translate—τῷ πλήθει τῶν Πλαταιῶν οὐ βουλομένῳ ἦν τῶν Ἀθηναίων ἀφίστασθαι. ὤφελες ζῆν.

9. Translate—Nobody appeared either on the wall or at the gates; how would they ever arrive if they sailed in a contrary direction (εἰς τἀναντία)?

133.

1. Parse γεγῶσα, κατακτάς, ηὐξῆσθαι, πτῆναι, ἀφείθησαν.

2. English of ποῖ, ποί, πότερος, πού, ὅθεν, οἷ.

3. Give six Futures Middle having a Passive meaning.

4. Distinguish πάρεις, παρείς. φασί, φᾶσι. νέων, νεῶν.

5. Decline in Sing. πλέως.

6. Give examples of the-Accusative Absolute.

7. Principal Tenses of τρέφω, τρέχω, ἁλίσκομαι.

8. Translate (with Notes)—οὐκ ἔφασαν ἑκόντες εἶναι προδόται ἔσεσθαι τῆς Ἑλλάδος. τὶ ἐμποδὼν μὴ οὐκ ἀποθανεῖν ἐμέ;

9. Translate—Tegea all but revolted; I don't know whether I shall be doing right; he said he would do nothing against the laws.

134.

1. Explain Enclitic. Name the chief Enclitic words.

2. Parse ἐσθῆτι, ᾅδης, ἔπη, σπῶμαι, ἐῴκειν.

3. Distinguish the meaning of the Aorist from that of the Present in σιγάω, γελάω, πολεμέω, νοσέω.

4. When is μή used (1) with Participles, (2) with Infinitives ?

5. Show the constructions of ὅπως.

6. Write out Aorist Subj. Act. of δίδωμι, and Aorist Opt. Act. of πέμπω.

7. Show that the Article may have a Demonstrative force.

8. Translate (with Notes) — ἐκέλευεν ἥντινα βούλεται δύναμιν λαβόντα τὸ ἐπὶ σφᾶς εἶναι ἐπιχειρεῖν. ἀναμνήσω ὑμᾶς τὰ τούτῳ πεπραγμένα.

9. Translate—They said the king had sent them, bidding them ask why this was being done; they asked what they could do to please us (χαρίζομαι).

135.

1. Form Pres. Indic. from Stems τακ-, φθα-, σταγ-, ῥαγ-, θιγ-.

2. Decline in Plural ὑγιής.

3. What is noticeable in the forms θρέψω, ἠκούσθην, βέβληκα, ἤρκεσα, ἔφυν ?

4. Derive Iconoclast, Dyspeptic, Asbestos, Homœopathy, Comedy.

5. Show the uses of the Optative in Independent Sentences.

6. Parse ἀπηλλάχθαι, τεθναίη, πάθῃ, ἐπίστῳ,. ἐχύθη.

7. Distinguish Active and Middle meanings of γαμέω, ἵημι, σκοπέω, δανείζω.

8. Translate—He said that if he had had anything he would have given it; they reckoned that if they did not fight the allies would revolt.

9. Translate—Ἀργεῖοι δὲ καὶ αὐτοὶ ἔτι ἐν πολλῷ πλέιονι αἰτίᾳ εἶχον τοὺς σπεισαμένους ἄνευ τοῦ πλήθους, νομίζοντες κἀκεινοι μὴ σφίσι πότε κάλλιον παρασχὸν Λακεδαιμονίους διαπεφευγέναι.

136.

1. Show the construction of τιμωρέω, Act. and Middle.

2. Give six Transitive Verbs in which the Perfect has an Intransitive meaning.

3. Distinguish ὅσοι μὴ λέγουσι, ὅσοι οὐ φασι. ὅτε, ἔπει. οὔτε, οὐδε.

4. Parse ἦρα, πένητας, ἥβης, ἤσκει, ἐπισπόμενοι.

5. Gen. Sing., Gender and English of ὄχλος, σκάφος, σκιά, σῦριγξ, ὀφρύς.

6. Accent λαβε, ποιησαι, δουναι, ταχθηναι,. κομισαι, ἐφιλει, ἐτιμων.

7. Comment on the forms ἐλήλακα, ἔστραμμαι, κομιῶ, ἡρέθην.

8. Translate—The calamity is too great to bear; they asked him with what object he was acting thus.

9. Translate (with Notes)—οὐκ οἶσθα μοίρας ἧς τυχεῖν αὐτὴν χρεών ; πείσομαι γὰρ οὐ τοσοῦτον, οὐδὲν ὥστε μὴ οὐ καλῶς θανεῖν.

137.

1. Show the force of the Termination in σποράδην, γραφεύς, νεανίσκος, ἰσότης, βαρύνω.

2. Give Active and Middle meanings of ἔχω, τίθημι (νόμον), γεύω, βουλεύω, αἱρέω.

3. Show the various meanings and uses of ὡς.

4. Decline γέρας in Sing., νεώς in Plural.

5. Distinguish ἐδηλοῦ, ἐδήλου. ἀγγεῖλαι, ἄγγειλαι. οἴκοι, οἶκοι.

6. Mention Compound Verbs taking Augment both before and after the Preposition.

7. Perf. Pass. of αἰδέομαι, καλέω, τιτρώσκω, μιμνήσκω, τέμνω.

8. Translate—πολλοῦ δεῖ οὕτως ἔχειν. ἐκ δακρύων γελᾶν. εὖ πράττειν. μείζων ἢ κατ' ἄνθρωπον.

9. Translate—While the supper is being pre-

pared, we will remain here; he said he wished to know who were present.

138.

1. Parse ἀξιοῖς, σκέψει, ἀπόκριναι, εἰωθυῖα.

2. Name ten Feminine words in -ος, Second Declension.

3. Derive and give meaning of αἰχμάλωτος, πανουργία, μεσημβρία, ψηφίζομαι, μοῖρα.

4. Give the meaning of ἔρρωγα, λείψομαι, ᾠήθην, ἐγρήγορα, μέμνημαι, διελέχθην.

5. Accent ἀγαθον τι. λογος τις. λογοι τινες. ὁρω τινας. εἰ τις τι σοι φησι.

6. Classify the forms of a Conditional Sentence.

7. Explain the forms γένος, λύων, μείζων, θάσσων.

8. Translate—οὐκ ὅπως ἐκώλυσεν ἀλλὰ αὐτὸς ἡγεμὼν γεγένηται. οὐ μὴ γένηται τοῦτο. μὴ τοῦτο ἀληθὲς ᾖ.

9. Translate—Reckon no man happy before he is dead: you could not do it if you wished.

139.

1. Write out Aorist Indic. and Imperative Act. of γιγνώσκω.

2. Parse ᾔδει, ἥδε, ἦρε, ἦρι, ἤρατο, ἠρᾶτο.

G*

3. How may a Wish be expressed in Greek?

4. Decline in Sing. πλέως, in Plural πρᾶος.

5. Principal Tenses of μεθίημι, ἀμφιέννυμι, χέω.

6. Distinguish νέων, νεῶν. οὔκουν, οὐκοῦν. εἰ, ἐάν. πῶς, πώς.

7. Explain the uses of μὴ and οὐ.

8. Translate—οὐκ εἶδεν οὐδείς. ἐπαινῶ οἷόν σε ἄνδρα. ἔφθην ἀφικόμενος. ἤρετο τίνος δεόμενος ἥκοι. φεύγειν φόνου.

9. Translate—I am not afraid that this will happen; they were not strong enough to open the gates; if you had not done this, you would not now be suffering.

140.

1. Write out Fut. Indic. of βιβάζω, and Aorist Subj. Act. of δίδωμι.

2. Classify the chief uses of the Subjunctive.

3. Derive and trace the present meaning of Philippic, Diploma, Cynosure, Archipelago.

4. Illustrate the use of the Reflexives σφᾶς and αὑτούς.

5. Form Adverbs from κρύπτω, ὀνομάζω, ῥᾶστος, χείρων.

6. Parse in two or more ways δηλοῖ, ἵστη, τιμῶσι, ποιήσει.

7. Explain Cognate Accusative and Accusative of Respect.

8. Translate—There is nowhere for me to flee to; I have a right to do this; we are faring well.

9. Translate (with Notes)—μάλιστα οἶμαι ἂν σοῦ πυθέσθαι. ἐν τοῖς πρῶτοι Ἀθηναῖοι τὸν σίδηρον κατέθεντο.